WHISPERS OF WANDERLUST

Short Stories from Diverse Lands

M.O. Raghunath

Compiler & Editor

GULF BOOK SERVICES

**GULF BOOK
SERVICES**

Published by Gulf Book Services Ltd
20 - 22 Wenlock Road, London,
NI 7GU, UK
Email: info@gulfbooks.co.uk
SPCFZ, Sharjah – UAE

First Published by Gulf Book Services Ltd

ISBN: 978-1-917529-18-1
Year: May 2025

Illustrations: Hannah Dennis, Bahman Ashrat Bharucha, Drishti Jain, Anushka Shah, Laranya Gupta, Saesha Kapoor, Dhriti Attavar, Ananya Mehta, Sreya Nair, Hanaya Ahuja (Students - GEMS Modern Academy, Dubai), Ganga Raghunath & Ishan Raghunath (Students-GEMS Our Own Indian School, Dubai)

Cover: Grace Dennis (DP 1 student, GEMS Modern Academy, Dubai)

Typeset in Garamond by Madhavi.S, Forging Minds, India

FOREWORD

It is with a sense of privilege that I introduce Whispers of Wanderlust, a remarkable anthology that transcends borders and brings together voices from across the world. Through the mesmerizing stories, a testament to the beauty of cultural exchange, a celebration of diversity, and a tribute to the boundless creativity of young storytellers, Raghunath has masterfully woven a tapestry that will leave you spellbound.

At GEMS Education, we believe in fostering curiosity, embracing global perspectives, and inspiring a love for learning that goes way beyond the confines of the classroom. This collection of 66 short stories written by students studying in educational institutions across 60 countries embodies the spirit of imagination, diversity, love for learning and more, offering readers an opportunity to explore unfamiliar traditions and experiences through the lens of young authors who have poured their hearts into these narratives..

Our world is interconnected in more ways than ever before, and literature serves as a powerful bridge that celebrates us despite our differences. It allows us to peek into the lives of strangers who soon become familiar to us through their joys, challenges, and aspirations. The young authors adeptly take you on a journey across six continents where you will savor the unique flavor of a culture you might not be familiar with and revel in the universal emotions that bind us together.

Heartfelt congratulations to Raghunath! Your dedication and vision in bringing this project to life is remarkable. Your passion for literature, education, and global collaboration has been the driving force behind this extraordinary initiative. It has been wonderful to witness your commitment to curating this unique collection.

A project of this magnitude demands the involvement of many, and I cannot help but appreciate all those whose contributions have made this book a reality — student authors, illustrators, library professionals, educators, take a bow! You have played a vital role in making Raghunath's dream a reality - *Whispers of Wanderlust*. What a labor of love this has been. Bravo!

Nargish Khambatta
Principal-GEMS Modern Academy
Senior Vice-President-Education
GEMS Education

BEYOND BORDERS: A CELEBRATION OF CULTURAL NARRATIVES

Wanderlust is intrinsic to human nature, causing inherent restlessness, shaping the history of humanity through perpetual movement across seas, mountains and forests. This journey has given rise to, shaped, and divided nations, continents, and territories. People tried to establish and re-establish themselves and frequently succeeded in doing so in different places. Consequently, diverse cultures and heritages have flourished alongside the nomadic histories, a narrative that persists to this day.

Nothing else compares to the unique power of art, literature and music to accurately capture people's culture and heritage. It appeals to people across the world, breaks barriers and unites them as humankind living on the same planet.

For a long time, it has been my dream to use the art of storytelling to introduce readers to the diverse customs, histories and everyday lives of people from all over the world and this book promises one such amazing experience. My endeavor here was to encapsulate such a concept within the pages of a book, aiming to touch the hearts of readers in a unique way. Regardless of the hemisphere, the language, the latitude and longitude, what unites us is our humanness- our emotions and values that remain the same. I am sure that the unfamiliar histories and cultures will enrich the readers' thoughts and enhance their experiences, guiding them through captivating narratives. In these pages, the magic of discovering the history as well as cultures of other countries through the innocent eyes of children have been captured.

My years in education as a library professional as well as my engagement in numerous international conferences within the field have not only shaped my aspirations profoundly but have also allowed me to build strong connections with library professionals across the globe. Their unwavering and invaluable support, especially from the IASL leadership and its members, has been crucial as I embarked on this initiative. I am also grateful for the tremendous support extended by Mrs. Nargish Khambatta, Principal and Vice-President, GEMS Education, throughout this project.

Several individuals have played crucial roles in encouraging and supporting this endeavor, particularly my colleagues and friends who assisted in sourcing short stories for this project. As the compiler and editor, I extend my heartfelt gratitude to them. Their unwavering support has been indispensable, and without it, this endeavor would not have come to fruition as seamlessly as envisioned.

This book, consisting of 66 short stories from 60 countries spread across 6 continents, is the first students' short story collection in the world with unique cultural representation from the country they live in. As we delve into these stories, it becomes evident that many are inspired by the real-life experiences of the student authors themselves.

I am very happy that I was able to initiate this and successfully bring it to the readers. Leveraging the power of technology and social media along with constant support from all those who helped me with this, the project reached its successful fruition in approximately one and half years. With great pride, I present this collection of stories to readers worldwide.

In today's world of Chat GPT and other AI tools, it gives me immense pride and joy to acknowledge the heartfelt 'authentic and original work' of these young authors who have painstakingly scripted, edited and revised their stories several times. Kudos to the young and promising authors-- the future of the world!

Thanks & Regards,
M.O. Raghunath

CONTENTS

A Day just like any other in Trelew

Guadalupe Longueira Caldas (Cumelén)
Grade 9
San Leonardo Murialdo High School
Adrogue, Argentina

I got up very early, as always, and the first thing I did was to prepare a good and bitter *mates.*[1]

I like watching the sunrise while I drink it. When the sea is calm and the tide is high, it is easier to see the whales.

My house is on the outskirts of the city and there are not many houses around. It is a quiet place to live with lot of native fauna. In the mornings, birds are always singing, and sometimes some felines such as the pumas or foxes go by my garden; the only ones that don´t get closer are the *choiques*[2]

It was quite pleasant to wake up on a day like that one, when the weather was hot, and the sun was shining. I usually go to the coast by bike but that day I thought it would take too long, so I decided to go by car and reduce the time. In twenty minutes, I had arrived at Rawson Port, near the Union Beach. I arrived, parked, took the field glasses and got on a motorboat. I usually rent one to go offshore to get a closer glimpse of the whales, although I'm not always lucky enough.

It was November, so it wouldn´t be difficult to spot these beautiful marine creatures that have fascinated me since I was a child.

Here, southern right whales can be found. Each year, they come to get pregnant with their pups, which come back when they are ready to hear the "cultural transmission" delivered by their mothers. This

---

1. *The "mate" is a traditional drink in Argentina, shared with other countries of South America, in which in a kind of bowl, "yerba mate" is put, then hot water, but not boiled, and through a "bombilla" that filters the yerba, water is sucked to be drink.*

2. *Word used to refer to the Darwin´s rhea.*

transmission is not innate but taught to the next generation. There are also orcas and toninas. Already in the open sea, in the distance, I could see penguins on the shore; those Magellanic penguins that are no more than half a meter high. Together with them, there were other colossal animals like sea wolves, elephants and lions.

The ocean was calm, the early morning was coming to an end. In the distance, the splash of those whales' enormous bodies on the water could be heard. I began to get closer and closer; I was excited about getting to touch them – that soft and viscose skin that reminded me of the moments I was lucky to see them so near. However, it scared me a bit as they went by the side of my boat. Such big creatures, jumping and emerging on the surface, can give the impression that they may hurt your boat or yourself, or the feeling of not knowing exactly when they were going to appear.

Just then, something strange happened: a whale calf got closer, making its characteristic noises, hitting the boat insistently. It went back and came again calling for my attention. So I decided to follow it. It took me directly to the Union Beach. From far, I could only see a huge shape in the shore. As I got closer, I noticed that it was a whale. I brought the motorboat closer to the shore and went to ask for help. I called the Argentine Environmental Police and they answered me that they'd come soon.

I was desperate. It was so early that there was no one that could have found her before I did. I was afraid it was too late, and I was even more afraid of the fact that I didn't know for how long she had been stuck there and for how long her calf had been restless, begging for some help. How long had she been in this position? How long could she stay in that place? Questions only invaded my head and I was overwhelmed by despair.

When they arrived, I was able to calm down a little, and so began the hard task of carrying her to the sea again. The calf, out to sea, was nervously expecting her arrival. It took twenty-four hours to successfully return the whale to her place. A crane, nets, and almost thirty-five people, including me, trying to help. Others just went by to take pictures. Some stood still and left helpless. Later, more people started to come to rescue her.

And in a moment a big cry of joy from everyone was heard, including the whale who began to exhale strongly, getting us even wetter, when she was finally freed. Then, we enjoyed watching her, jumping with its characteristic whale breaks in the water.

After taking pictures of her and her calf enjoying the open sea, I came back to the shore. I got into the car and turned the key with its respective keychain with a shark and a Carnotaurus. Since I was a child, I've loved both, and being in the museum boosts my wish to keep investigating them.

I got home, took a shower, grabbed my bag, and went to work, this time by bike. I worked at Trelew's downtown, in the "MEF" (Egidio Feruglio Paleontological Museum). It's a place with important complete and incomplete findings of big dinosaurs. At the Museum, fossils, dinosaur models, and their evolution can be found. Also, skeletons of some big prehistoric mammals, such as mammoths and moose are exhibited, paleontology of invertebrates and vertebrates is studied, as well as paleobotany. My job is to check if all the pieces are in their place, and to go to excavation sites to find new specimens.

I arrived exhausted at my workplace. One of my best friends said to me:

- "Che[3]! Look at your face! I heard about the whale. How are you about that? "

Sighing, I answered:

- "It was a long day. I slept a little. But well, I had to come to work. Although the fact of being tired doesn't take from me the pride of having helped to save the whale."

---

3. *"Che", it's a word used in Argentina to call someone's attention.*

The House on Murray Street

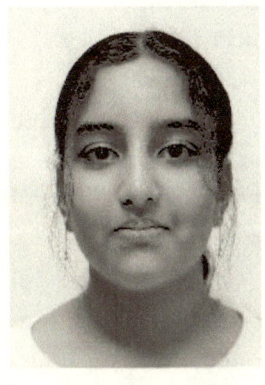

Dhwani Vimal
Grade 5
Goonawarra Primary School
Melbourne, Victoria, Australia

The girl turned and ran, shrieking as she went faster and faster, her breath coming in ragged gasps. Sweat dripped down her forehead, her heart hammering like a war drum. Her name was Lilly. And right now, she was lost in the deep, tangled bushland outside Mornington, Victoria, fleeing into the unknown.

Lilly pushed past towering eucalyptus trees, their twisted branches reaching like fingers in the moonlight. Dry leaves crunched underfoot, and the scent of damp earth filled her nostrils. After what felt like hours, she stumbled to a stop, bracing herself against a gum tree covered in peeling bark and stubborn moss. Her legs shook, and she slumped onto the cool grass, her chest heaving as she tried to piece together what had just happened.

It had all started that afternoon when she and her brother, Levi, were walking home from school, their backpacks bouncing on their shoulders.

"Hey, Lil, do you know about the haunted house down on Murray Street?" Levi asked, his voice brimming with excitement. "I heard it's actually scary."

Lilly had simply shrugged. She wasn't one for ghost stories. That night, however, she found herself reluctantly following Levi down the deserted street, the warm evening air thick with the scent of wattle and salt from the nearby coast.

They reached the house without trouble. It was a weathered old Queenslander, its verandah sagging, paint peeling, and iron roof rusted like an old Holden left to the elements. The garden was overgrown with spiky lantana, and gnarled gum trees stood like sentinels around the eerie structure. A twisted path led to a heavy wooden door, its brass knocker tarnished with age.

Levi, always the brave one, strode up and knocked. "Anyone home?" he called.

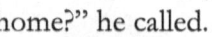

Silence.

Levi turned away, rolling his eyes. "Guess it's just an old story—"

Before he could finish, the door burst open, and a thick, grey mist poured out. Lilly coughed and blinked as the fog curled around her, and then—

Levi screamed.

She barely had time to register the sound before he was yanked inside, the door slamming shut with a thunderous bang. "LEVI!" she shrieked, pounding on the door. Smoke hissed from the cracks, and an unnatural chill seeped into her bones. Then, instinct took over. She turned and bolted, sprinting blindly until she reached the bush.

Now, lost and alone, tears stung her eyes. She had abandoned her brother. What kind of sister was she?

"Hey… Hey, kid…"

A raspy voice cut through the silence. Lilly jolted upright to see an old man standing before her, his leathery skin tanned from years under the harsh Aussie sun. His scruffy beard was flecked with grey, and his Akubra hat sat at a lopsided angle. He smelled of eucalyptus and campfire smoke.

"You look like a roo caught in the headlights," he said, his bushy eyebrows furrowed. "What are you doing out here, love?"

Lilly swallowed hard. "My brother… He's trapped in that house on Murray Street! Please, you've got to help me!"

The man rubbed his chin thoughtfully. "My name's Barnie. I reckon we'd best check it out, then."

Lilly hesitated but then nodded. She had to be brave. For Levi.

The two made their way back to the house. The eerie glow of the porch light flickered as if sensing their return. Barnie placed a calloused hand on Lilly's shoulder. "Stay close, kiddo."

He pushed open the door. The smoky mist curled around their ankles as they stepped inside. The house groaned like an old dingo waking from sleep. Shadows twisted along the walls, and the air smelled of dust and something rotten.

"Levi!" Lilly called. Her voice echoed, swallowed by the oppressive silence.

Then—movement.

A figure emerged from the dark. Levi stood in the center of the room, his face pale, eyes wide. But something was wrong. His limbs jerked unnaturally, as though pulled by invisible strings.

"He's not alone," Barnie muttered, gripping a wooden boomerang hanging from the wall. "Stay back, Lilly."

A guttural growl rumbled through the room, and a shadow shifted behind Levi. A tall, gangly figure emerged—a bunyip, its eyes glowing like embers, its wiry limbs creaking as it moved.

Barney acted fast. He threw the boomerang, and it whizzed through the air, striking the creature's chest. The Bunyip let out a bone-chilling shriek as it recoiled, its form flickering like a dying flame. Levi collapsed to the ground, coughing. Lilly dashed to him, shaking his shoulders.

"Levi! Wake up!"

He gasped, his eyes focusing on her. "Lilly…?"

Barnie grabbed them both by the arms. "No time for reunions, let's skedaddle!"

The three sprinted out of the house just as the walls began to shake. The Bunyip howled in fury, its form twisting and vanishing into the mist. As they reached the road, the house let out one final groan before crumbling into itself, vanishing into the night like it had never been there.

Levi coughed, shaking his head. "What... what happened?"

Lilly hugged him tightly. "You scared the hell out of me, that's what!"

Barnie chuckled, adjusting his hat. "Well, I reckon that's enough adventure for one night."

The siblings exchanged a look, then nodded.

As the first rays of morning stretched over the horizon, the three walked away from the ruins of the house, leaving the horrors of the night behind. But deep in the bush, among the rustling gum trees, a whisper carried on the wind - a chilling reminder that some legends never die.

Twin Bonds and Furry Friend -
The Story of Ollie

Amal & Aarav
Grade 5
No.132-134 Educational complex
(IB School)
Baku, Azerbaijan

This is the story of Ollie, our four-legged companion. But it is not just Ollie's story; it is also a tale of natural beauty and heritage of our country.

We are identical twins, and it is difficult for our friends and relatives to recognize us. Only our father and mother can easily distinguish between us. However, there is another who has come to recognize and understand us and our antics - Ollie, our Uncle Jacob's dog! Uncle Jacob is our neighbour and a friend of our parents.

We live in Baku, the capital of Azerbaijan. Our father is Indian, and our mother is Azerbaijani. When our grandparents came from India, they too initially struggled to recognize us. After spending a few days together, they began to understand us. However, by then, it was time for them to return home.

Whenever our grandparents visit, a local tour is a usual activity. It is during these trips that they get the chance to understand us better and observe our inconsistencies.

During these journeys, we get more knowledge about our respective homeland Azerbaijan and father's country India. At bedtime, grandma tells some Indian folktales too. Grandma would impart the first lessons about our country, and a beautiful country nestled near Russia, Iran, Turkey, Georgia, and Armenia. Then slowly would disclose some stories about the beauty and religious harmony of India, especially Kerala.

Grandma would often inquire further, directing questions to our parents and the guides accompanying us on the trip, while Grandfather would meticulously capture the beauty of the moments through his camera lens. Most of the information what we discovered was lovingly shared by Grandma, occasionally supplemented by insights from Grandpa. While Grandma would extol the country's natural beauty and prowess in sports, it was Grandpa who enlightened us about Azerbaijan's treasures, such as the Gobustan State Reserve archaeological monuments, the world's largest number of mud volcanoes, and its abundant oil reserves.

Now, let's talk about Ollie. Our neighbor, Uncle Jacob's dog, Ollie, holds a special place in our hearts. Uncle Jacob and Aunt Binu reside in a large villa near our house and are close friends of our parents. Every day after school, we would toss our bags on the table and dash to Uncle Jacob's house to play with Ollie, a delightful English Cocker Spaniel who relishes the cool Azerbaijani weather.

Ollie adores having guests and showers affection upon everyone, but he feels melancholic when they depart. He is remarkably obedient, dutifully following Uncle Jacob's commands, which often prompts our parents to half-jokingly urge us to learn from Ollie's obedience.

Ollie's main playground is behind Uncle's grassy backyard, where he enjoys playing with us. His enthusiasm knows no bounds when we arrive, and our favorite pastime is playing ball with him.

However, Ollie has a peculiar aversion to crows, barking at them whenever they appear. When Uncle tends to the birds in the backyard, Ollie's demeanor transforms, becoming serene and composed.

In addition to Ollie, Uncle Jacob's house is also home to three large turtles, which Ollie adores. They seem at ease only in his presence, retracting into their shells when we approach.

On our journeys, Ollie accompanies us. During that time, Ollie will be rested on Aunt Binu's lap while she affectionately strokes his head and neck. Ollie loves sweets, but Aunt Binu never promotes it because she fears it may affect his health.

If we narrate a small incident that happened during such a trip, that will help understand how much Auntie cares for him. That incident was on our Gabala trip a few months ago.

One memorable outing took us to Gabala Falls and Lake View last winter. During the trip, we ate snacks in the car, which Ollie eyed longingly. Sensing his desire, we gave him some sweet biscuits and chips. But Aunt Binu found this trick! At that time, aunt gently discouraged and warned us. She said that it was only for Ollie's well-being.

It was one of the memorable local tours because of the long journey from Baku as well as the cable car experience through the Gabala mountain. The rides up the hill and the steep descent from there were very interesting. Uncle Jacob enlightened us about the region's beauty and historical significance of Gabala. As we marveled at the sights, Uncle Jacob explained that Gabala, situated approximately 225 km from Baku, was amidst the southern slopes of the Greater Caucasus mountains and was renowned for its natural splendor and historical importance.

We thoroughly enjoyed the waterfall and lake views. One thing we observed was that, just like in Baku, Gabala also had a lot of tourists.

When Uncle told us that Azerbaijan's natural beauty and climate attracted tourists from all over the world, and that's why it had so many people that day, we felt proud of our country. Amma added that tourism is also an important source of income for Azerbaijan.

There was another incident in Ollie's story. Ollie doesn't like Uncle and Aunty going anywhere. Once, when uncle and aunt were packing a box to go to India to see their unwell father, he did something at night. He gnawed the wheels of their box. He thought that if he did so, they would not leave him. But they entrusted him to the care of the servants and bid him farewell.

After a week, Uncle and Aunt returned from India. Upon their return, we visited Uncle's house, eagerly anticipating a grand welcome with Ollie running towards us as usual. However, there was no such thing! Moreover, he was nowhere to be seen in that area. It hurt us deeply. The gravity of the situation became apparent only when we reached the yard of the house. There, we found him lying unconscious in the backyard.

Autumn in Azerbaijan is also the season of pomegranates and apples. It was during this time that my uncle and aunt went to the countryside. Ollie didn't receive enough attention while they were away. Uncle Jacob attributed his illness to eating too many things, including apples.

Don't you know he only needs to have one apple a day?" Uncle looked at the workers and asked.

"We used to let him play. A lot of apples had fallen last night. He ate a lot of them. We didn't think he would do this, Sab," they said.

As his best friends, we know that Ollie likes apples very much. Every day was like an apple ration. Now that he had a chance, Ollie took it gladly and ate as many apples as he could. It made him sick.

When the vet came and administered the necessary medication to Ollie, he recovered within a few days. Now, we continue with our usual playtime activities…

A Journey Back to My Kindergarten Classroom

Noela Sarwar
Grade 10
DPS STS
Dhaka, Bangladesh

My mind was full of thoughts, my feelings were like a fast-moving ride, and everything around me felt messy and confusing. The big, difficult words on the board jumped around like dancers. I could not understand them because they were new to me. The bright white walls shone with fresh paint, and colorful papers covered the softboards, just like cars crowding the streets of Dhaka.

My kindergarten teacher looked at me with sharp eyes. I pretended to pay attention in class, but my eyes showed that I was lost. When my teacher asked me a question, I stood up nervously. I tried to say the Bengali alphabets but failed, making the whole class burst into laughter.

The classroom had maps of Bangladesh, and just by looking at them, I felt like I had to travel from there! I closed my eyes. In my mind, I explored the deep green forests of Chittagong, walked on the longest beach in Saint Martin, and imagined the ancient ruins of Mahasthangarh, where kings once ruled. I eagerly set out on a journey to the village in Sylhet. Riding the launch across the vast Padma River, I watched fishermen casting their nets, their songs blending with the rhythmic splash of water.

When I finally reached an unknown village, the aroma of freshly made 'pitha', a traditional Bengali rice cake, filled the air. Over the next few days, I explored the lush green paddy fields, listened to Baul music played on an ektara, and joined the villagers in a colorful 'Pohela Boishakh' festival. There, the people treated me to a delicious meal with hilsa fish curry. I felt a deep connection to Bangladesh's rich traditions—its hospitality, its flavors, its music, and its unwavering spirit. As I dreamt of magical places, my teacher's rhymes played in the background.

I was full of curiosity, always asking questions and drawing whatever came to my mind. My crayons helped me create a world of my own, filling my notebook with bright colors. Some children argued over paintbrushes, some tried to impress the teacher with facts, and others proudly showed off their drawings. The most talented ones drew "Nakshi Katha," a special embroidered blanket made by village women. These blankets told stories—of farmers playing flutes, cows grazing in the fields, and women carrying water from the peaceful Padma River.

Then, the lunch bell rang. "Ring! Ring! Ring!" Everyone excitedly opened their lunch boxes, their eyes sparkling with delight. The air was filled with delicious smells—sweet sauces, tasty meat, and spicy curries. My lunch was a simple omelet on warm, flavorful "khichuri" (a delicious mix of rice, lentils, and spices). The spicy, tangy taste made me feel calm and happy, as if I had taken a bite of paradise. I giggled with my friends, chatting about our favorite cartoons.

Suddenly, I felt someone smash on my back. Startled, I turned around and saw my mother's face. That is when I realized—I had been dreaming!

She smiled and shook her head. "Were you daydreaming again? You came home from school and have not even eaten yet," she said before leaving the room. I sat there for a moment, still lost in the vivid images of my dream, before finally getting up to join her.

I thought about my Kindergarten days. Life felt so simple and fun back then. I loved touching the smooth wooden chairs, feeling the paint on my hands, and enjoying the simple things around me. Kindergarten was a time when school did not feel heavy, and we were not stressed about deadlines or studies. Back then, happiness was found in the smallest things. Thinking about it now, I wish I could go back—to that happy, colorful classroom, far away from the world of high school.

The Whistler

Santosh Mourao Thomas
UFOPA, Santarem
Amazon, Brazil

The story I'm going to tell are memories of my grandmother, who was born in Vila Socorro, Lago Grande, a distant village from the city of Santarem, on the banks of the Amazon River. In the Amazon, most of the communities live in the river side and they depend on water for their livelihood. The only way to reach the village is by a small boat. It takes a whole day to reach the village by river.

Many people say that this entity exists.... you'll know if it's true. Nobody disbelieves that.

It was December – the time when the river started to flood and don't you know there are only two seasons: summer, the time when

the river goes down, because it doesn't rain and the rainy season which runs from December to May – and grandma Edineusa was expecting to go and spend the birthday of her brother Jone, who lives in Vila Socorro. She was looking forward to seeing her brother again, as she had lived in Santarém for many years. And so, she left, happy because she would find her roots again.

When she arrived at the village, it was already night, Joné, his wife and other relatives were happily waiting for her. As a custom, she had taken a lot of presents from the city to give her relatives. Ater the supper, Edineusa didn't want to sleep in the house, she preferred to sleep in a hammock in a longhouse with other family members, where she could talk and catch up with latest happening in the community.

The gossip was too many and they didn´t know the time passing. It was almost midnight when the whistles started.

- Is it the porpoise, who is whistling, wanting to date a girl? – Joné asked.

- No, after all there is no puxirum (community gathering). Edineusa replied.

Her sister-in-law Irene stated:

- But you, huh? Don't you know the difference between a porpoise's whistle and a whistler's whistle? That's the whistler. I've known the sound since I was a child. Likes to scare people. Some say it is the mother of the forest; others say it is the Curupira, the protector of the forest.

And so, Irene continued her narrative:

- Once the whistler scared a cousin of mine, who to this day doesn't go into the woods, he stopped hunting. He liked to hunt capybara. But that day, it was already dark, he heard a whistle, but he had no idea it was the entity. He ran after his prey. When the animal was in the sights of his rifle, he noticed a figure and then felt his body on the ground and a deafening whistle. He soon remembered the stories his mother told him about the protector of the forest, Curupira, a small boy, with red hair, sharp teeth and feet facing backwards who disorients hunters using his deafening whistles and his footsteps in reverse. The cousin started running, terrified, screaming for help.

There was silence.

- It's not better to go in, to sleep, away from that whistler. It's not good to discredit. And tomorrow I want to eat that fish stew and the "bolinha de piracuí" to celebrate Joné's birthday. Edineusa said.

- It's better not to disbelieve, said Joné.

My Family Reunion

Kenfack Talla Manuella Clara
Grade 12
Enko La Gaiete International School
Yaounde, Cameroon

Every year in the month of August, a family reunion is done in my village. This date was chosen because it was my grandfather's birthday. My grandfather was the family's leader and one of the notables (Chief's advisors) of the chief.

The name of my village is Bameka. It is in the western region of Cameroon. In Cameroon, Twins are said to have magical powers and the fun fact is that my name is Kenfack which means "Twins' little sister" in my mother's mother tongue.

The family reunion has been done for as long as I can remember. Every year, at around end July, all the kids and even the parents giggle and fidget about how the event will be for that year. Who will be there? What will they bring for us as gifts? How will they travel? And many other questions. I was about six years old, and that was the first time I was going to be at the family reunion. We did a family road trip together with my cousins. It took about 7 hours because we lived in the capital of the Country (Yaoundé), located in at the central Region of Cameroon. During the road trip, we stopped at 'Makenene' which is a well-known eating place. We were so happy! We ate Chicken, pork meat, braised plums and plantains and Wild meat such as Giant rats. After that, we went to buy gifts for everyone and drove straight to the village.

Upon arrival, I was amazed! There were trees all over, fresh air, few houses, everyone was friendly, and most importantly, my grandfather's house was HUGE! A lot of people were already in the village, aunties, uncles, cousins, and even the elders. We were warmly welcomed, and the atmosphere was jovial. A lot of us did not know each other, but we barely did 10 minutes that we were already running everywhere! We were then asked by the elders to change ourselves first and eat before playing. After we ate, all the kids were asked to go to the farm to harvest what we will return home with. It was my first time going to the farm. I was very excited. We picked up polypropylene bags and bamboo baskets together with hoes and cutlasses and all in the direction of the farm! Both adults and kids. Before reaching the farm, we passed through a sacred place called the small "Noh" which is a place where rituals are done for our ancestors.

We arrived at the farm and harvested a lot of ground nuts and maize. In between the maize trees, we occasionally found tiny Irish and potatoes. We were kids! We obviously took advantage of the situation to play in the fresh red soil. We even made use of creativity and constructed houses with maize tree stems and ground nut leaves. We laughed a lot and had so much fun. We went home all dirty like little pigs! All the kids were washed up by aunties using a sponge made of polypropylene sac. It was a bit rough, but it washed very clean. After bathing us, our heads were shaved with blades and oil was added to make it as shiny as crystal balls. We were given empty top parties cap to wear. When you looked at us, all that you could see were dwarfs with shining semi-circle with a bright mark left by the reflection of sun light on them. It was hilarious!

We played, danced, and told stories till about mid-night around the fire. We were more than forty in number, and more were expected to join us. We ran around my grandfather's mansion, made up of about eight houses, looking for a place to sleep. There were no rooms left for us. A huge waterproof tarpaulin was installed on the floor and many kids including me slept there under a huge cover sheet. It was more comfortable than I thought. Next morning, we woke up by six. All the kids were asked to rush to the Noh (sacred place). Upon arrival at its entry, sweets were thrown to the sky by the elders, and the kids rushed to pick them. I was very strong, so I picked a lot. We then entered the Noh.

It was dark, calm, and humid with giant trees and sounds from animals such as wild birds. In the heart of the Noh, a goat was sacrificed to the ancestors by the elder men, a fire was lighted using woods from the forest and the goat was roasted by them. It was then cut into pieces and was immersed in a container filled with red palm oil and salt was sprinkled upon. Beside the meat was a huge basin of boiled rice and a bucket of ground nut soup. We were all asked to line up and receive the meat with our bare hands. We had to take it with both hands to show respect to the elders. After the meat was eaten, we were to eat the rice and soup on top. It was delicious!

I remember asking myself, "How are we going to eat without any dishes!"

Before I could finish thinking, I saw all the kids diving their hands into the huge basin of rice. They ate so fast! And those that were slow would just carry the rice with both hands out of the basin and eat gently. By the time I realised, it was almost finish. I almost cried. Fortunately for me, my father had kept his own meal apart as all the elders did. I ate more comfortably. Gallons of oil and bags of salt were also kept apart for the grandmas (no one was left out). After the Noh, we all went to the river to swim. We only swam in the small middle portion because at both sides, the currents were too heavy. We organized a swimming competition, with the price being food! We loved food! We also did a bit of laundry.

After coming out of the water, we were all white like chalk with red eyes like little wizards. We played even harder in the courtyard at my grandfather's house. We played football, cat game, hide and seek and even fighting games. We had mud all over us! I remember my uncle had just arrived with gifts for all. We were all very dirty and ran to greet him.

He said "Look at you piglets! Go wash up or else you will receive no gift!"

We executed his command. We carried water from the well and went to bath. The well was more than 25 metres deep and had a 10 litres bucket attached. We had to pull more than 50 buckets both for people and for laundry, so took turns. In the chaos, my cousin fell in there. We dragged him out with the 10 litres bucket attached to the well. It was the eve of the main day.

At the lunch hall, the meat was left to cook all night till the fire died under it. It was then cooked in a huge traditional pot together with raw plantains, capable of feeding about a 100 people, it was the main course.

The morning of the Reunion was very busy. We had a lot to do. We had to cook other dishes, such as rice, tomato soup, chicken, goat, pears, plums, etc. We also cleaned and cleared the grass all-round the mansion and did a last jump to the farm. The night of the Reunion, we were all wearing our nicest clothes, kids like adults. Huge stands and chairs were placed at my grandfather's main house. There was a jovial mood. Music, food, drinks and even neighbours were there. It was one of the greatest events in the village. The elders shouted "Punange-Pon" meaning "You are all welcome" and we all answered "Òh, Òh".

All kids presented themselves with the grade they were promoted to. Juice was shared to kids and liquor to adults. My Grandpa did a speech and later there were financial contributions by the adults. After that, the most important part was lunch. The food! We all ate till our stomachs were about to explode. The meat, which was the most important meal, specially cooked by my grandpa in his house was the yummiest! We then danced, did competitions and did story telling beyond mid night. The next morning was time to part our ways. All what we harvested was equally distributed by my grandma even though some people had kept their harvest for themselves. Grandpa and Grandma said their final words. They parcelled food to eat on the way. We said goodbye to everyone with a sad face holding incredible memories.

We did not have the chance to see the traditional Jujus such as "the Le" which are very frightening and run after people to hit them or the "Nian nian", the twins, who are as shiny as the sun. No one can take photos of them. If someone tries his/her camera breaks unless he is a twin like them.

In Loving Memory of Grandpa.

Is there Anything you are Afraid of?

Taleen Salam Aljubori
Grade 4
Kingsview Village Junior Public School
Toronto, Canada

Hey there, I'm Olivia, and I'm in grade three at my primary school. I call the vibrant city of Toronto in Canada, 'My home, sweet home'. My days are ordinary, filled with activities I love like swimming, drawing, biking, and skiing. But there's one thing that makes me nervous – heights.

Living in Toronto means being surrounded by towering buildings and skyscrapers. Sometimes, I shy away from places that others find stunning. I get jittery looking out windows that overlook concrete jungles and busy streets crammed with cars. My family adores dining at restaurants on high floors with glass balconies boasting panoramic city views. It baffles me how they can enjoy such sights when they terrify me.

My city, Toronto, is one of the most beautiful cities in the world and is renowned for its skyscrapers. As the capital of the province of Ontario, Toronto is a major Canadian city situated along the northwestern shore of Lake Ontario. This dynamic metropolis boasts a core of towering skyscrapers, all overshadowed by the iconic, free-standing CN Tower!"

On the day of my birthday, my parents planned a sightseeing trip for me before the birthday party. Dad had given me some choices too. What will I choose? As you know, Canada is famous for its gorgeous scenery and vast, depopulated land. There are three oceans, mountains, plains, and some of the most attractive cities in the world. However, the sights of the beautiful and natural environment are mostly untouched by humans or tourists.

It's my eighth birthday. My mom insisted we celebrate the day on the top floor of one of the biggest restaurants. I dug my heels in, refusing adamantly. It was embarrassing to admit my fear, but with some prodding from my parents, I spilled the beans. Heights make me uneasy, and I don't find them beautiful at all. Mom started reminding

me of my bravery – how I fearlessly dive into deep waters and zip down ski slopes. Dad chimed in, saying, 'Remember, bravery isn't the absence of fear; it's controlling it.'

At their favorite spot, Mom coaxed me to sit by the window, holding my hand gently. 'Try focusing on the heights and ignore the ground below,' she said. 'Talk about things you love.' That's when it hit me – I love drawing. I saw it as a chance to sketch this breathtaking view. Usually, my artwork features trees and water, but now it captures towering structures and the play of light and shadow.

I took those small steps to conquer my fears and embrace the beauty of parks, waterways, and skyscrapers around me. Now it's your turn. Do you have any fears? Can you face them head-on and take control?

A Crystal Amethyst

Kanishka
Grade 7,
AISG
Guangzhou, China

I walk up the stairs. My calves burning, my thighs aching.

But it feels good.

It feels good to avoid the paparazzi, the cameras, the constant questions, and the spotlight.

However, I could do without the itchy wig on my head and the bandanna that I used to cover my face so no one could recognize me.

All for a few days away from the celebrity life.

People occasionally stare at me, but most give me warm smiles and wave to me. Some kids point and laugh in delight. Very different from back home where people would trample me to take photos. While I love the support and attention, it can be a little bit overwhelming. This break was much needed.

The Great Wall of China.

So strong and sturdy yet built centuries ago using sticky rice glue.

I smile at the thought.

Just then I bump into someone, I turn around to find a frail, old woman looking up at me.

"Oh! I'm so sorry Mam, I didn't see you there."

She smiles, "That's okay, my girl. What are you doing around here? You seem troubled by thought." She says, her accent and broken English making it hard to understand, but I get what she's saying so much as I can answer the question.

"Tell me about it. I'm here on a…hiatus. My old life was overwhelming, and I was stressed. I just got out of a terrible relationship and barely got out of a 'crazy – fan – murder – scheme'."

She lets out a low whistle and I chuckle.

"Just a regular day in the life of an all-time famous singer."

At that, she smiles, "You know, though I don't know exactly what you're talking about, if I know one thing for sure, it's that you should keep going. Don't stop for one stalker or because of haters. You do it for you."

"I Love that. Thank you, mam."

"Don't mind me asking, but why you come here? To Great Wall of China?" Her brows furrow in confusion and she manages to push out the final words.

I chuckle, "Well, my mom is Chinese, and I grew up mostly in Beijing, that's before I moved to the States and my career took off. I feel like I lost touch with the place that made me who I am today. So, I took a month hiatus and decided to come back and be in touch with my culture and my background. I figured the Great Wall of China would be perfect for that."

"That's wonderful, my girl. But what is hiatus?"

"Oh, it's when you take a break from regular practice. In this case, it was taking a break from my regular life to explore my childhood."

She smiles a small smile, one that almost makes it seem like she is smiling to herself.

"Well, honey. You are doing great. I don't know you, or your history, but I know you doing great. You know, the Great Wall of China is a symbol of strength and unity. You push through, and you will make it. You got that, my girl?" She asks.

I smile. And it's the realest smile I have smiled in a while.

"Thank you so much, Mam. I needed to hear that. You are...?" I ask, hoping I can at least catch her name before she leaves.

"No Mam, call me Lin. Aunty Lin."

"Well, it was great meeting you, Aunty Lin. I hope we cross paths again." I say a spark of hope in my voice.

"Of course, my girl, what is your name?" She asks, her eyebrows raised.

"Mei. Mei Yu."

Her face lights up.

"I knew there was something familiar about you. My granddaughter loves you, but I have weak memory, I couldn't tell if it was you. I even went to you concert with my granddaughter once, you are amazing."

I chuckle, delighted. Then, I remembered something.

I opened my purse and took out 2 of the tickets with backstage passes to my next concert.

"Here! I keep these with me for my fans. I hope to see you and your sweet girl their next time, Aunty Lin."

"Oh my gosh! We will be there. We will be there, and we will cheer louder than everybody else.

I grinned. But just before I turned away, she told me to wait.

I spun my head to look at her, "Yes?"

She reaches into the worn Tote bag on her shoulder and pulls out a...Crystal?

"Here, this for you. I had it for too long and my days are long over. Now, I want you to have it."

I give her a puzzled expression.

"This is Amethyst, my girl. It gets rid of your negative energy and promotes your wealth. Has a soothing energy and can help you think more clearly."

My mouth opened in surprise. "That honestly sounds like everything I've been needing lately. But I still can't take it from you, that is too much."

"No, no", She insisted. "You have already done something so special for me and my granddaughter. This is least I can do. Here, take it." And then she pushes it in my hand and balls up my fingers to create a fist.

I grinned at her again, "Thank you. Thank you so much."

"Of course, my girl."

And then she gave my hand a reassuring squeeze and turned away, I did the same.

As I walked away, I could feel the strength of walking on the Great Wall of China seeping into my body. I hoped for my life to be great again.

I think about Aunty Lin, how the stranger who is now a friend and mentor has possibly changed my entire career, heck, maybe my whole life.

I squeeze the amethyst still balled up in my fist, feeling hope and clarity finally coming through to me.

At the end of it all, I smile.

A Dance of Colors and Memories

Natalia Rojas
Grade 10
Colegio Los nogales
Bogota, Columbia

In the busy and lively city of Barranquilla, where the scent of ripe mangos overwhelmed your senses and the sound of laughter filled the streets, there was a young girl named Sofia. Sofia had grown up hearing stories of the extravagant Barranquilla Carnival from her mom. She was told how her grandmother, and her dad spent their life and energy on the carnival before their sudden death in a terrible car accident. Her mom always told her how the Barranquilla carnival was a celebration that brought together the rich fusion of Colombian culture in a dazzling display of cumbia, salsa, and champeta music, dance, and vibrant costumes. The Barranquilla Carnival is a vibrant cultural celebration in Colombia and the preparations run for a whole year. It is renowned for its colorful parades, music, dance, and folklore, serving as a symbol of Colombian identity and unity.

One sunny morning, as the city buzzed with excitement and anticipation; after preparing the carnival for the whole year, the week of the carnival had finally arrived. Sofia felt a stirring in her heart, with a sense of wonder and adventure. She made her way to the heart of the carnival, her eyes wide with anticipation and her spirit soaring with excitement. With each step she took, Sofia felt as though she was embarking on a journey through Colombia's diverse landscapes and traditions. She marveled at the rhythmic movements of the dancers, whose graceful motions told tales of love, passion, and resilience passed down through generations.

Mesmerized by the colors and sounds that surrounded her, Sofia felt as though she had stepped into a world of pure magic. Everywhere she looked, she saw costumes that told stories of Colombia's rich cultural heritage—elaborate dresses adorned with intricate embroidery, vibrant masks that evoked the spirit of ancient rituals, and headdresses adorned with feathers that danced in the breeze, Sofia stumbled upon an odd costume stall tucked away in a secluded corner. Among the dazzling array of outfits, one costume caught her eye—A beautiful feathered sparkling dress with the colors of the Colombian flag. At the top, delicate orchids cascaded gradually as they descended, creating a stunning look.

Unable to resist the appeal of the costume, Sofia eagerly took the dress, feeling a strange tingling sensation as she wore the dress. Suddenly, the world around her became blurry and shifted, and before she knew it, Sofia found herself traveling through time and space, landing in 1918 in the midst of a bustling street filled with vibrant colors and lively music.

Confused but still determined, Sofia set out to explore her surroundings, marveling at the sights and sounds of one of the past Barranquilla Carnivals. As Sofia wandered through the past Barranquilla Carnival, she encountered a young, beautiful woman amidst the festivities. Her beauty was captivating, her presence commanding attention as she moved gracefully through the crowd. There was an air of regality about her, and Sofia couldn't help but feel drawn to her. At that moment, Sofia realized that she was in the presence of the queen of the carnival Alicia Lafaurie Roncallo—a symbol of grace, beauty, and strength embodying the spirit of Barranquilla's vibrant celebration, soon she discovered.

However, as Sofia gazed upon the radiant carnival queen, a sense of familiarity washed over her—a feeling deep in her heart that she couldn't quite place. It was as if she had known this woman her entire life, though she couldn't recall ever having met her before. Even though she was eager to go speak to her, Sofia was paralyzed with her emotions, she couldn't process everything at once. She saw a young boy approaching the queen, a very handsome little boy, with green eyes and a beautiful smile. She instantly felt a connection with both of them, almost if they were like family, however, she couldn't quite put her finger on it.

Sofia started to feel weird, the world around her became blurry and shifted, she couldn't shake off the feeling from the journey, as if it held a deeper purpose—one that went beyond mere chance or coincidence. And when she finally arrived back in the present, she stood perplexed amidst the familiar sights and sounds of the Barranquilla Carnival in the heart of the city of Barranquilla. She rushed home to her mom Mara. She wanted to know everything about the past carnivals.

Maria's eyes sparkled with excitement as Sofia eagerly listened to her mother's words. "Mija[1]," Maria began, her voice filled with emotion, "Your dad and grandma, they loved the carnival more than anything else in the world. They would spend hours preparing for it, sewing costumes, practicing dances, and immersing themselves in the vibrant culture of Barranquilla." Sofia's heart fluttered with a mixture of surprise and joy as she absorbed her mother's words. Could it be possible that the mysterious woman she had encountered in the past carnival was her own grandmother?

Maria continued, her voice trembling with emotion. "Alicia Lafaurie Roncallo, the first queen of the carnival, was not just a symbol of Barranquilla's celebration. She was your grandmother, Sofia." Tears welled up in Sofia's eyes as she embraced her mother tightly, feeling a deep sense of connection and belonging wash over her. It was as if the pieces of her past had finally fallen into place, revealing a story that was intertwined with the rich tapestry of Barranquilla's carnival history.

1.Mija- *Literally meaning "my daughter," mija is used as a familiar and affectionate address to women, like "dear" or "honey," in Spanish.*

When books sleep

Magdalena Burul
Grade 7
Elementary school Vladimira Nazora
Potpićan
Potpićan, Croatia

Stillness. Great silence. Everything is sleeping in Zagreb city. In the large city library, books small, large, thin, fat fell into a deep sleep.

The night was cold and rainy. A big, strong wind swayed the city library building. With the huge gust of wind, a book fell from the third-row shelf.

Oh, she fell alone, and I hit myself hard," said the Little Mermaid. "I'm scared, I'm cold.

"No one heard. She began to sob softly. But, in the last row of the library, at the end of the last shelf, The Lion King suddenly woke up from sleep. "What is this?" he asked loudly. "Who dared to wake me up like that late at night? Is anyone there?" continued the lion. The little mermaid softly whispers: "I fell, I'm very strong to hit myself. I guess I didn't break anything".

The lion king decided to see what is happening in the middle of the night, and who sobbed so quietly. He saw a tiny, fragile Little Mermaid on the floor. She was so helpless, but unusually beautiful. The Lion King had never seen such a small and delicate creature in his life.

He gently picked up the mermaid with his big paws and warmed her with his fur.

"Oh! Thank you!"

The Little Mermaid uttered and then looked at the lion in the eyes She saw great power, courage and strength, but most of all kindness and tenderness. She felt safe and warm. Neither felt helpless nor lonely, anymore. At that moment, their eyes met and from that moment they were inseparable. The lion looked at the Little Mermaid and spoke: "You know, little one, if you have faith, hope and good luck, then you will find love. And you will be happy all your life." They laughed and the two of them stood in the middle of the library, holding each other. The other books woke up and started to applaud them.

The Lion King requested the Little Mermaid to accompany him. They both went out of the library and watched the beauty of Zagreb city. The trees beside the roads welcomed them to the city. The plants showered their flowers on them and showed their happiness.

They realized that the expansion of Zagreb city proceeded eastward and westward. They saw the new residential construction that went up on the south (right) bank of the Sava River. The north of Medvednica Hill was visible from the city. The hills in the Zagorje region of woodlands, vineyards, picturesque villages, and ancient chateaus were appalling to their eyes. They saw, many old constructions like the Gothic-style Church of St. Marcus and the former Jesuit monastery. The lion and the little mermaid walked back to the library satisfied, after their extraordinary city tour and the wonderful experience.

The next morning, everything was quiet. Zagreb city was ready for its gallop! The library opened; it was full of children who loved to read books. Suddenly, in the third row of the library, a little girl named Stella appeared and chose the Little Mermaid book. The lion rebelled a little and got worried for the mermaid. But he knew that it was their duty to let the children choose their books.

Books serve to make people, especially children, beautify the world and create an imagination in which they live. The Little Mermaid came back after a few days and lived happily with her lion, in the big city library, on the third row of the shelf. They were separated for good when someone decided to read them.

Little Karl's Fastelavn

Jonathan Basil
Grade 6
Per Gyrum School, Nivaa
Copenhagen, Denmark

It was a beautiful spring morning in a little town called Nivå, in the north of Copenhagen. The sun was shining, the birds were singing in a beautiful tone, and the flowers were blooming. The warm spring air was slowly entering the calm and peaceful town of Niva, the town of nine streams.

Little Karl was still in bed while his mother was talking to her friend on the phone. "Oh, really, Ida? It sounds like a good offer for the Fastelavn's pastries this year!" Hearing this, Karl jumped out of bed and ran to his calendar. With a shout of joy, little Karl realized that tomorrow was going to be Fastelavn, his favorite celebration. Every Fastelavn day reminds him of the old traditions that his grandma once told him. As per Christianity, in Denmark, Fastelavn marks the first day of the forty days of lent before Easter.

His grandma told him that a few hundred years ago, people used to put a black cat in a barrel and hit the barrel until the cat was dead! The black cats symbolized evil witches. It was a little scary for Karl. But nowadays, at school, kids dress up in different costumes, decorate the barrel with cats cut out of black paper, and fill it with sweets. He was so excited; he couldn't wait to hit the barrel and become the cat king this year. Karl had missed becoming the cat king the previous year.

He ran to check his costume cabinet. He found his ninja costume, but he had already worn it two times. Then he found his pirate costume, which didn't fit him anymore. Finally, he found his Spider-Man suit, which was missing an eye. "Oh no, I have no costume for Fastelavn!" Karl ran to his mother for help. "Mom, I have no costume for Fastelavn tomorrow!" exclaimed Karl. "Well, have you checked your cabinet?" asked Mom. "Yes!" said Karl. "Alright, then let's try to buy a new one," said mom. So, Karl hopped into mom's car, and they drove to Copenhagen Center.

At Copenhagen Center, Karl and Mom went into a costume shop. There, they found loads of costumes and props. "Would you like to be an elf?" asked Mom. "No," replied Karl. "How about a doctor?" asked Mom. "Nope," said Karl. "Hmm, what about a firefighter?" "Umm, I think not," said Karl. Finally, Mom pulled out a costume from the rack. "What about a Viking?" The costume had beautiful fur armor and a perfect helmet with big, curving horns. It even came with a long foam sword. It was perfect. "Oh yes, please, mom," said Karl gleefully. They went to the counter to pay for the costume.

Karl was so happy until he heard the worst thing ever. The shopkeeper said that the Viking costume was reserved. "Well, are there any more like this one?" asked Mom. Karl looked up with hope in his eyes. "Sorry, ma'am, they are all sold out," said the shopkeeper. "Oh well, thanks for the help anyway," said mom. Karl and Mom went back to the car and drove home. The car ride was very silent. Nobody spoke. At home, Karl went up to his room. He could see the others all happy with their costumes. They were running around with their costumes, playing, and having fun. Little Karl was sad that he couldn't join in because he didn't have a costume. Karl curled up in bed and started crying. But he knew that it wouldn't help. Suddenly, there was a knock on the door.

Karl went to see who it was. There, standing at the door with a bag and a box from the bakers, was dad. "Hi dad," said Karl sadly. "What's in that box?" asked Karl. "Oh, I went to the bakers to find some pastries," said Dad. "I also stopped by the costume shop to pick up a costume," said Dad. "Costume? Which Costume?" I asked a curious Karl. Dad showed Karl the costume. It had fur armor, a helmet with big, curving horns, and a long foam sword. Karl recognized the costume and was immediately filled with joy. He ran to hug his dad. He smiled and cheered. "But Dad, how did you get the costume?" asked Karl. "I reserved it," said Dad. "It was you who reserved it?" asked Karl. "Yeah," replied Dad. Karl was very happy. He thanked his father. Then he ran off to play with his friends.

Scary day in Moucha Island

Netanya Sam
Grade 6
International School of Africa
Djibouti

The Incident I Would Never Forget! It was a nice, sunny day. The sail from Djibouti City to Moucha Island would take 40 minutes. That day, we headed to Moucha Island, and it was amazing. We had a nice swim in the sea and had a lot of fun there. We enjoyed some delicious food and made sandcastles, but before we could finish, the sea waves came and destroyed them. However, the terrifying event was yet to come.

OH, I forgot to introduce myself!

I am Nadia. My home is in Djibouti City, the capital of Djibouti, a country in the Horn of Africa. This Arabic and French-speaking city stands out in many ways. Most of the people are Muslims in Djibouti. It is the youngest African country to gain independence from French colonial rule.

Djibouti City has its own unique charm. Filled with hills and mountains, it is a natural wonder. One notable feature is Assal Lake, which is said to be saltier than the Dead Sea. It is considered the world's most notable saltwater lake after Antarctica's Don Juan Pond and Gaet'ale Pond. Another peculiarity of Assal Lake is that salt is extracted from it for human consumption. You might wonder how a child like me knows all this. This isn't what I learned in school; it's what my father told me.

Moucha Island is the largest island in Djibouti and stands out among the country's natural wonders for various reasons. Known for its size, it is also a favorite destination for many people. The beauty and the opportunity for an adventurous boat ride were irresistible. That's why we chose to visit Moucha Island during the weekend, avoiding other places.

After enjoying at the island enough, we decided to head back to Djibouti City by 4:00 PM. As we were leaving Moucha Island, the sea became rough. After sailing for 10 minutes, the boat got stuck in the middle of the ocean due to an engine failure. The boat started drifting, and we were stranded, seeking help from other boats passing nearby. Unfortunately, they thought we were just waving at them. Finally, a boat with French military personnel came to our rescue. They towed our boat back to Djibouti City. It was a scary day.

The trip had a happy ending and thanks to the military scouts who saved us from drowning or becoming a meal for sharks. My parents were furious with the boat service team as they didn't have any life jackets on board. I encouraged my dad to file a complaint against them for not following the safety rules. We reported our concerns to the military officer, who promised to take our complaint seriously and inform the concerned department. The boat service could lose their license but not all might get help as we got, so we had to do what was right.

Despite the scare, I was excited that day. The main reason for my excitement was the complaint we submitted against the boat service team. Before we reached home in the evening, we enjoyed some more delicious food from the restaurant. I proudly shared all the incidents with my friends.

Whispers of Egypt: A Journey on a Paper Plane

Alia Abdellatif and Aisha Massoud
Grade 10
Capital International Schools
Cairo, Egypt

If you have to go to one place in Egypt; where could it be?" The youngster seals the letter and turns it into a paper plane. The winds are stronger near the deck of the cruise. Trekking through the tranquil waves, the cruise makes its way towards the first civilization. The plane is launched by the youngsters' curious grip. It flies towards the horizon as the wind takes it far away to a group of children playing at the corniche.

At the corniche, Laila is playing the exiting game of chase with police officers chasing the robbers, a game well known to Egyptian children. The paper plane lands on Laila as she runs along the Corniche—the coast of the Mediterranean—while the wind blows through her hair. She smiles brightly as her friend makes a turn towards the fish market. Distracted and hungry, Laila can't help but eye the huge lobsters, shrimp, and crabs, all fresh and waiting to be haggled. Her friend calls her name as she runs through an alley, making her way to the Citadel of Qaitbay. The castle watches over the clam ocean as a parent does a child. The chase continues within the towering walls of the castle, within hundreds of years' worth of history. Laila chases her all the way to the lighthouse. There, the chase ends. Together, they climb the steps and stand on the edge of the lighthouse. They watch the sun as it makes its way, preparing for another day. "The ocean, the food, and the history. What more could a person want? "Alexandria, of course!" chirpily thinks Laila. "I am waiting for you in Alexandria." Laila launches the paper plane and watches as the wind takes it far away.

Nour research on her computer to kill time, and the plane lands from the window onto her lap. She opens it and reads the message. "Cairo, of course!" The bell rings as Nour takes an Uber to Tahrir Square, a landmark known for Egyptian resilience and the best Koshari Egypt can offer. Her friends gather in Madenti, where they play in the beautiful gardens all day. Once finished, they pass by the kiosk and buy an unfathomable number of snacks like ma'moal and sham' biscuits. They accompany their families as they take the bus over to the club just in time to watch the football match. They cheer for their favorite team, El-Ahly. "The convenience, the safety, and the technology. What more could a person want? I am waiting for you in Cairo." Nour goes to her apartment's balcony, launches the paper plane, and watches as the wind takes it far away.

Youssef rides his horse in the dunes of Giza as he catches the paper plane; he reads the message.

"Giza, of course!" He gets off his white Egyptian horse and walks towards the oriental outdoor seating. Youssef draws a pot of Arabian coffee for his parents as he waits for the water to boil for his tea. He sits down and takes in the contrast of the yellow desert and the blue sky. Once done with the tea, he calls a chariot to take him to see the Great Pyramids. He puts on his red and white keffiyeh and investigates the many mysteries hiding within the pyramids. He studies tombs and walls and tries to read the hieroglyphics. The sunset finds Youssef standing atop the pyramid.

"The Great Pyramids, the best tea, and the warm sun. What more could a person want? I am waiting for you in Giza." Youssef closes the paper plane and launches it; the wind takes it far, far away.

Raghab eats Fiteer for breakfast. He savors its sweet taste as he reads the message. "Fayoum, of course!" After a hearty breakfast, Raghab heads to the local pottery shop for his daily lessons. He molds the brown clay beneath his fingers. Slowly but surely, he makes it into the shape of a cup. After leaving it to dry in the oven, he heads to Lake Qarun. Raghab gets on the felucca along with his friends. The boat floats through the body of water. The boys swim in the cooling water, which washes away the heat of the desert sun. Once finished, they ride beach buggies along the lake and between the grass fields. Raghab admires the greenery as they drive to a sand dune. There, they do sandboarding until their legs ache. Raghab stargazes as he writes. "The lake, pottery, and endless activities. What more could a person want? I am waiting for you in Fayoum." Raghab walks to the highest peak of the dune and throws the paper plane; the wind takes it far away.

Yassen wakes up a bit after sunrise, and his family's rooster crows. As he feeds the farm animals, he reads the message. "Saeed, of course!" He pets a dog as he walks to the cows. He pours them water and heads back home. There he eats a traditional Egyptian breakfast: scrambled eggs with tomatoes, mashed beans, falafel, molasses, and tahini, and Egyptian country bread (baladi). With a full belly, he and his friends decide to play football. After winning the match, Yassen decides to wrestle with them in between the grass. He leads the group to a man-made lake, where they all swim for a while. As the sun begins to set, they go pray their evening prayer at the mosque. Once completed, Yassen heads to the rooftop of his home, where he writes, "A filling breakfast, never-ending fun, and lifelong friends. What more could a person want? I am waiting for you in Saeed." Standing on the edge of the roof, Yasseen throws the paper plane, and the wind takes it far away.

Ayah starts her day by wearing her colorful veil. "Siwa, of course." She laughs. Ayah and her few friends go to the oasis and the Salt Lake, where she farms some salt to be sold. After some time, she rides on her camel and returns to the remaining Bedouins. There, Ayah teaches tourists how to ride camels and horses. She and her friends collect an assortment of shells and rocks, and they use the materials to build beautiful necklaces. They then advertise their merchandise to the tourists. At midday, she accompanies her brother on a safari. Ayah sees unique dune formations, rare birds, and breathtaking views. They stop at the sand bathing area, where people from the entire world come to heal themselves. Ayah climbs up on the safari car and holds the paper in her hand. "Hospitality, unforgettable experiences, and culture. What more could a person want? I am waiting for you in Siwa." Ayah launches the paper plane, and the wind takes it far, far away.

The youngster's parents share a glance. They laugh, holding the letter in their hands: "It seems our trip to Egypt will be longer than expected." The youngster looks confused. "We must go everywhere." They throw the paper plane for the last time, and the wind takes it far, far away.

The Night of Bonfire and Flowers

Anushree Vinodkumar
Grade 10
Greek Community School
Addis Ababa, Ethiopia

One quiet Saturday night, I sat alone, surrounded by shadows and silence, in my bedroom in Addis Ababa, the capital city nestled in the Ethiopian highlands. The room, dimly lit by a flickering bulb, echoed with the weight of my thoughts. My heart was heavy, overwhelmed with a mixture of emotions: depression, distress, and a deep sorrow. My parents had made the final decision. We were leaving Ethiopia. Moving to a foreign land with unfamiliar skies, unfamiliar streets, and unfamiliar smiles.

Outside, the cool, calm air of the evening had settled as it often does in Addis nights. I could hear faint echoes of Amharic songs playing in the neighborhood. The sound of life around me contrasted sharply with the stillness I felt inside. My room was a mess. Partially packed suitcases full of clothes, memories, and emotions, lay open on the floor. I curled up and let sleep take me into a world more alive than my waking one.

In the dream, I found myself lying on a soft, spongy couch in our living room. Suddenly, the sharp ring of the doorbell jolted me awake. Curious, I opened the door to find Selam our dear friend from the house next door. Her warm smile lit up her face.

"Selam, betam des yilign! What a surprise!" I said.

"Enamesegenallo! I'm here to invite you to our Meskel celebration tonight!" she beamed, her white Habesha shawl gracefully draped over her shoulders.

I stood there stunned. How could I forget? Today was Meskel, one of the most vibrant and spiritually significant festivals of Ethiopia, celebrated in memory of the finding of the True Cross by Empress Helena in the fourth century.

I ran down with her to their compound. The air outside was festive, filled with laughter, music, and the delicious aroma of spices. My neighbour's yard, like many others across the country, was transformed, well-decorated for the occasion. In the centre, stood a towering Damera—a pyramid-shaped bonfire made of eucalyptus branches collected from the Entoto hills, tied with yellow Adey Abeba, Ethiopia's symbolic flower that blooms during the New Year.

People gathered around, dressed in their finest traditional Habesha Kemis decorated with elaborate golden embroidery. The spiritual chorus of "Meskel Mezmur" filled the air, echoing through the compound and ascending into the star-speckled night.

Selam took me to the coffee ceremony corner, where her grandmother was roasting fresh buna beans over hot coals. The scent was intoxicating, a rich aroma that was more than just coffee. It was tradition, love, and home. Next to her were large bowls of kolo and freshly popped popcorn, which are always served during such ceremonies. The rhythmic clinking of tiny porcelain cups and the soft buzz of conversation filled the air.

Then came the moment. The Damera was lit, its flames reaching upward, symbolizing triumph of light over darkness and faith over doubt. Selam and her family began to dance around the fire. The kids formed circles, holding hands, laughing and singing. The older women clapped and ululated in joy. Teenage girls moved gracefully to the rhythm of Eskista, a traditional Ethiopian dance known for its expressive shoulder movements, set to the beat of drums and krar music.

Later, Selam's mother called us in for dinner. I stepped into the kitchen, where the rich, appetizing smell of Doro Wat, the fiery chicken stew spiced with berbere and enriched with boiled eggs, filled the air. Next to it, Kitfo, minced raw beef seasoned with mitmita and niter kibbeh, glistened beside bowls of Gomen or collard greens. All of it was served on injera, a sour flatbread, laid out on a big plate to be shared between all members. Each bite was rich, full of flavor, and heavenly. It remained in me as an unforgettable memory.

As we stepped outside again, the last embers of the Damera crackled under the dark sky. Smoke drifted upward, carrying with it the laughter, love, and blessings of the night. Ashes floated like fireflies, and for a moment, the world felt timeless.

Then...

The music faded. The light dimmed. The aromas disappeared. I heard a distant ringing, a sound soft, yet, persistent.

I blinked.

Suddenly, it was morning.

The spinning blades of the old ceiling fan above my head creaked gently. The golden morning light poured through the curtains. The packed suitcases in the corner reminded me of what was real. A taxi honked outside, ready to take us to Bole International Airport.

Was it a dream? Or was it my soul's way of saying goodbye?

That dream—or maybe that memory—was Ethiopia's final gift to me. It reminded me that I belonged to more than one place, that home is not just where you live, but where your heart finds its rhythm. Ethiopia, with its mountains and music, coffee and culture, became a second motherland. A land that shaped me, loved me, and whispered, "You'll always be one of us."

Beyond Borders: A Kaleidoscope of a Young Girl's life

Chinamayi
Grade 8
Oulu International School
Oulu, Finland

Life brings along all sorts of uncertainties. After experiencing a few, we think that there's nothing we haven't seen and that we are 100% prepared for anything and everything that's thrown our way. However, I learned that this is almost never the case. I'm a 14-year-old teen, and this is my story of how I finally came to terms with, well, my life.

I have lived in many countries over the last thirteen years. I quickly adapted to various cultures in my life because I lived in an international community, which taught me to silently blend in with the crowd. Sure, I stood out. People looked at me differently because of my accent and behavior, but I always controlled how much I stood out—enough to indulge in the attention but blended enough to still be considered one of them. I might not have felt that I was like them, but that didn't matter to me.

During the summer of my 4th grade, my mom told me, "Honey, I got a job offer in Europe. We might move there." It was like being able to see it in color for the first time. My world lit up. In March the next year, my mom, my sister, and I immigrated to Europe. It was great. I was 9 at that time, and I had lived in the Arabian countries for the past six or seven years.

Finland's northernmost region is called 'Lapland'. Almost all of Lapland lies above the Arctic Circle. In northernmost Finland, the sun just circles the sky all day and all night. I witnessed the midnight sun during summer. I played in lots of snow. I tried skiing and skating for the first time.

The first year went by quickly in Finland. I became more immersed in sports. My school seemed great too. I didn't have many Indian friends because there weren't many kids my age in the first place. Rather, my best friends were Nigerian, Libyan, Tanzanian, Spanish, English—the list went on. I felt like I was in my happy place again, in an international community where everyone looked different, where we were united not only by our similarities but also by what made us different.

When you go out of your comfort zone or to a new place, you drift towards people of your "own" kind. The thing is, I never felt that way toward any single group of people. That's why I felt most comfortable and accepted -among people like me—kids with an international upbringing, kids who didn't see skin color as a barrier. Sure, my fellow Indians looked like me, so there was that. However, like I mentioned before, I never felt that skin color separated me from someone else in any way. Well, that was until things took a turn for the worse, and I started seeing past the illusion of everyone being open-minded and accepting me for who I am.

My close friends started leaving school and even the country, and I had to find other friends. Obviously, this wasn't a problem for the social butterfly that I was. I adopted local European friends. I wanted to get to know the culture better. I was overjoyed that they liked me and saw me as one of them. In the beginning, it was all sunshine and rainbows.

Having them as friends felt different compared to my other Western friends. When I first came to Finland, they were secluded amongst themselves. It made me curious because they wouldn't interact with anyone else, particularly newcomers. This was the moment that I first started changing. Anyways, I loved hanging out with them, and we did all kinds of things that I'd never done before—go shopping, do skincare, and a lot of other 'cool' and 'exciting' things.

I would say that the confidence could have gone into my head. Like I said, my mindset after meeting these people was changing. We would gossip amongst ourselves. I started subconsciously feeling entitled and would push my other friends away. During the first period of our friendship, when I would share my culture and experiences, they would be met with fascination, praise, and appreciation. In return, they would share their own experiences. But as time went on, this started with slight changes. I got scared that they wouldn't accept me and that I had to change myself because, obviously, I'm the one with the problem. And so, I would instead do the things that I thought they found normal. I pushed all my other friends away to dedicate myself only to these people.

I think that you may have already caught on to what happened. I lost myself. The cheery, confident girl in me vanished. This process took a long time, and it's not something that happened overnight. By the time I realized that there was something wrong with what I was doing and the people I was surrounding myself with, it was too late. I ended my friendship with them. It hurt. The cold reality of everything shook me. I went down a toxic rabbit hole of hating everything that made me, me, feeling inferior to others and bowing my head to them.

It took a long time, about a year, to heal. I don't blame my friends now. I don't blame myself. Everything that happened was meant to happen. For a long time, I assumed that the world was great. Just because I didn't see people differently because of their skin color or ways didn't mean everyone is like that. I didn't learn this the easy or healthy way.

I convinced myself that I am worth as much as others and I should not be ashamed of myself. It's peculiar to think that I started off as the exact opposite person. Yet, surrounding myself with the wrong people led me to drastically change my mindset. I'm a stronger and wiser person now. I'm going to continue to grow and learn.

I felt like I was being open-minded by saying that I'm prepared and can take anything. But really, I wasn't. I was so fixed on the idea that I was such an adaptable and strong person whom nobody could deter, that I didn't even notice the way I changed until I was in the thick of it. Instead, now, wherever I go, I question myself, 'Am I doing the right thing? Is there something I can do better?'

Now, I observe my surroundings constantly and adapt my thinking. I've accepted that I'm a good person like others, but I can always get better; there's always room for improvement. Don't consider nationality or skin color. Adopt a learning mindset—learn from your mistakes, learn from your successes, learn from your enemies, learn from your friends, learn from yourself. Learn, learn, learn.

The Violets

Hanaé Laude Ouadah
Grade 10
Lycée Victor Duruy
Paris, France

It was an evening of heavy rain. It had rained suddenly in the capital, dripping down the Haussmanian Grand Boulevards and catching pedestrians and shopkeepers off guard. It was a cold, scathing rain, making stalls fly in the wind and umbrellas turn upside down. It drummed heavily on the tin roof of the old Parisian building, producing a metallic din, seeping into the framework already swollen with humidity and oozing down the walls. A man in his early thirties was hunched over his desk, glasses on the end of his nose, and a cigarette in his mouth. He was staring angrily at an immaculate white sheet of paper amidst the mountain of paperwork, invoices, and erased drafts under which his desk was crumbling. Everything around him exuded poverty: the smell of bad tobacco, the mattress covered in stains and cigarette burns on the floor, and an old jar of chipped violets as decoration. His room was in the attic of an old building on the Rue Babylone. It was a narrow, low-ceilinged space where you had to keep your back bent to move around.

He hadn't been out for three days (or was it four?) and spent his days in the stifling atmosphere of his garret, filling in drafts with ideas he thought were revolutionary. Then, on rereading them, he'd found each one worse than the last and ended up throwing it all away. A dull fatigue rumbled inside him, growing a little more every moment, weighing down his eyelids and clouding his thoughts. After a quick glance at his still hopelessly blank sheet of paper, he allowed himself a few moments of somnolence and rested his chin on his fist.

It was while staring at his bouquet of violets that he had his epiphany. He finally had the subject he'd been missing so much! He had it! He felt tears welling up in his eyes. His dream was at hand! It was inexplicable, but he felt it was the right one. He sensed that this subject would put an end to years of work and sacrifice for his writing. He immediately began to write feverishly on his paper, as if afraid that the subject would suddenly escape him. He wrote uninterruptedly for hours on end. He couldn't stop. With each line, his essay took shape—a perfect, indestructible form.

With each new word, he felt a little stronger, a little prouder, and a little more complete. He wrote relentlessly all night, smoking cigarette after cigarette. When the inky sky began to stain a pale pink, he was done. He'd written a good hundred pages in the space of one night. He didn't even know where he'd gotten all those pages from, so caught up was he in his writing, but it didn't matter. What he'd just done was a miracle - a pure miracle, he knew. Without even rereading his manuscript, he bound the bundle of sheets with a red string, which he kept for the occasion with the tenderness of a mother. Satisfied with himself and knowing exactly where he was going, he threw his shabby, patched coat over his shoulders, promising himself that a new overcoat would be his first investment once he was rich from the publication of his manuscript, and rushed out of his garret. He raced down the stairs with the reassuring weight of the manuscript against his heart. He emerged into the narrow Rue de Babylone, blinded by the morning light, and inhaled the capital's invigorating air. He then set off at a brisk pace, turning the corner of the majestic Boulevard des Invalides and continuing straight ahead to cross the Esplanade. He inhaled the fresh scent of dew on the grass on Avenue de Breteuil. He ran, flew, and crossed the still-sleeping capital in just a few strides. The spring drizzle was fresh and seemed to him to be more pleasant than the sun. He wanted to dance, to embrace the early-morning workers who were already crowding around him. He had his masterpiece!

Having already crossed the Seine and passed through the immense Louvre, he rushed into the first publishing house he came to and, without hesitation, with a blissful smile on his lips, handed his manuscript to anyone who wanted it. Without a glance, an old lady with skin more wrinkled than parchment coldly greeted him behind her desk and limply seized the product of his genius, but he was not offended. Surely, she was used to people who were sure of themselves, certain of having written a marvel, but, in reality, she was nothing more than a tissue of insipid, meaningless nonsense. She had the tired look of a woman who'd seen it all before, and nothing could impress her anymore. But he was confident. He knew he had something more. As the old editor's eyes scanned the lines, her expression changed. She went from questioning to genuine surprise, and she finished the page completely stunned. Stunned, she asked him if it was indeed his manuscript, and as he nodded arrogantly, she added that it was the most beautiful verse he had ever read.

The young poet felt a puff of pride grow in his chest. She told him, admiringly, that with such a feat, her success was assured, and she hurried to alert her superior. His reaction was identical. The faces of everyone who laid eyes on the verses lit up. Within a few weeks, the manuscript was printed, bound, and published, and it was an instant and monstrous success. His face was plastered everywhere, from the subway to the gigantic billboards overlooking the city. This new masterpiece was snapped up and described as a "child prodigy" and a "divine talent," with the most fanatical going so far as to describe him as a "literary messiah." The wildest names were attributed to him. And soon, the money started pouring in. He exchanged his elbow-length coat for an elegant tailcoat, his tapered bonnet for a top hat, and his garret for a comfortable apartment overlooking the Opéra Garnier. People started and turned as he passed. He left behind his unhealthy solitude as a tormented writer to go out in the evenings to the capital's most exclusive venues. He led a dream lifestyle - the one he had always deserved.

One afternoon, when the clouds were low and the atmosphere was heavy, while enjoying the luxury of his apartment, he glanced pensively at the huge bouquet of violets balanced on his desk. He smiled thoughtfully, fully satisfied with himself. He was happy. He chuckled to himself as he thought of all those failed writers with dried-up imaginations bent over their wretched manuscripts, filling sheets with bad rhymes that would never even come close to matching his immense work. He was deep in reverie when, all of a sudden, the scent of violets burst forth and filled his nostrils with a suffocating odor. He abruptly moved away from the bouquet, covering his nose, but the smell didn't dissipate. Where did it come from? With tears in his eyes, he threw himself at the window to try and open it. But, to his astonishment, the window refused to open. No matter how hard he shook it, the handle remained stubbornly closed. Worse still, the walls suddenly began to pitch dangerously, and the air became unbreathable. Before his horrified eyes, his living room began to warp, dent, transform, and curl until the walls were so stretched that he could no longer see the ceiling.

At the height of his horror, the proud writer almost turned a blind eye as they began to slowly advance towards him, trapping him. He fought tooth and nail, punching, kicking, screaming, and scratching, but the walls kept coming closer. He looked up at the sky and let out a long, agonized moan as the walls closed in on him for good.

He sat up, screaming, and opened his eyes in astonishment. It took him a few moments to realize the enormity of the situation. Around him, there was no comfortable apartment overlooking the opera, no opulent bouquet of fragrant violets, only a cramped, low-ceilinged garret with a filthy mattress on the floor and a jar of wilted violets in the corner. Tears stung his eyes. There was no huge poster advertising his work. No old publisher was in awe, just him and his needy imagination. O stupid, cruel dream! As empty and exhausted as a house after a fire, he slowly lowered his eyes to his sheet of paper, as insolent and immaculate as ever.

Christmas Market at Nuremberg

Nanda Sonilal
Grade 6
European School, Munich
Germany

When streets and market squares are transformed into a sea of lights; when the air is filled with the scent of gingerbread, baked apples, and roasted almonds—you know Christmas is around the corner.

Ring, ring, ring. Sophie's phone rang on Christmas Eve. It was a classmate, Amanda.

"Hey, Sophie! Have any plans for Christmas?" Sophie hadn't thought about that. She was too excited about Santa and presents, and had forgotten about the rest of the day.

"No," Sophie replied sheepishly. Amanda chuckled. "I felt the same last year until my mom's friend introduced us to visiting a Christmas market."

If someone else told her this, she would have fallen asleep that instant. But this was Amanda, and she was the opposite of boring. "A visit to a Christmas market is a must!" She continued.

"There are so many beautiful and enchanting regional handicrafts and festive delicacies. You should try the Christmas Punch; it is so good!"

"OK, let's start with the basics, shall we?" Sophie asked, "What exactly is a Christmas market?" Sophie was sure that Amanda must have raised an eyebrow because her tone suggested her surprise that Sophie had to ask.

"A Christmas market is a street market associated with the celebrations of Christmas during the four weeks of Advent. If you want to go, you should do so from November 29th to December 24th It is around those dates; they change every year!"

"Mum, Dad, this Christmas, can we go to a Christmas market?" Sophie said to her parents when later, she went downstairs. "Sounds

lovely, darling," said Mum. "Christmas market?" Sophie's sister Lilly questioned. "Since when did you want to go to a Christmas market? Tell you what, I'm not going. Staying out in the cold for hours and hours?" Lilly shivered. "Nope, not getting my hands and feet cold!" Lilly went upstairs to her room. "Lilly, come back!" Dad shouted. "You know what? Lily and I will stay home. If you want to go, you can go with your Mum. If she would like." He added quickly. Sophie looked at Mum. "So…" Sophie started. Mum smiled. "Yes."

Sophie and her mother decided to go to the Nürnberg (or Nuremberg in English) Christmas market. They decided to drive there from München. It was approximately a two-hour drive. Sophie opened her homework book. She had to read about Munich and answer some questions. "OK," Sophie thought, "let's get started!" 'Munich has monkish origins.' Sophie read. *The word 'Munich' derives from the Old High German term Munichen, which means 'by the monks.'* "I didn't know that!" Sophie thought, interested. *'Situated on the banks of the Isar River and north of the Alps, Munich is a top tourist attraction due to its geographical positioning. Munich is the birthplace of one of the most famous car brands, BMW, which stands for "Bayerische Motoren Werke" (Bavarian Motor Works). You can visit the BMW Museum, BMW Welt (BMW World), and the Deutsches Museum in Munich. Football is taken very seriously in Munich; their club, FC Bayern München, is highly famous and successful.'* "You know, I always had an interest in going to a Christmas market." Mum suddenly interrupted Sophie's reading. "I didn't go because none of you had any interest."

Mum sighed, then smiled softly. "Nuremberg's Christmas Market is called Christkindles Market. 'Christkind' is the gift-bringer for them." She explained. Sophie continued reading, '*Play Doh's birthplace, Munich! Pharmacist Franz Kolb's invention was intended for his artist friends, who had problems using modeling clay during cold months for their work.*'

Eventually, they reached Nuremberg Hauptmarkt, where everything caught Sophie's eye: stalls in bright colors, gigantic rides as bright as the sun, the smell—oh, how good it smelled! Caramelized nuts, cinnamon, so much cinnamon, and so much more. Sophie was breathless. She turned to her Mum in awe. "Wow." Sophie breathed. Mum just smiled. Mum took Sophie's hand, which was way warmer than hers, as they walked into Christkind's Christmas market.

late-covered bananas, an apple covered in chocolate and decorated like a mouse, and candy apples. "Can't eat another bite." Sophie panted. Mum arose, "We should get going if we want to get home by supper time." Before Mum was about to leave, Sophie shouted, "Wait!" and she ran off to one of the stalls. "Hi! Can I get something that Nürnberg invented?" The lady examined her. "Food or souvenir?" She asked. "Um…Food?" Sophie intoned. The lady nodded. "This is Nürnberg's gingerbread. The secret recipe for Nuremberg gingerbread has been handed down from generation to generation, and that's what makes it so special. I've added different flavors here; see which you like best." Sophie paid and thanked the lady before going back to Mum. Mum tilted her head when she saw the plastic bag of Nuremberg gingerbread. "A souvenir for Lilly and Dad," Sophie explained.

When Sophie and Mum reached home, they shared the gingerbread and told everyone everything that had happened. "So, I missed out on quite a bit," Lilly said when Sophie was done explaining. Dad looked like he regretted not going, and Lilly looked jealous. "Well, I suppose you had a lovely Christmas gift," Dad said. Everyone stood in confusion as Sophie shook her head. "One said," Sophie started, "the magic of Christmas never ends, and its greatest gifts are family and friends." Sophie grinned, "And I agree!"

Innocent Arrogance

Janell Miracle Tagoe
Grade 7
Association International School
Accra, Ghana

The blues of the sky divide the watercolor scene in two in front of my eyes. I see the horizon stretching out into the night, bringing a new morning. As I gaze outside the small length of glass, I laughably call a window, I can't help but be entranced by such a breathtaking view. The oranges, pinks, and yellows of the sky blend into a wonderful and chaotic clash of colors. The sea outside my window is the sight that greets me, reflecting the sky's magnificent light as if an angel were descending from heaven.

On the shore, I see fishermen hauling their slim boats onto the dock, getting ready for an early morning catch. It has long since become routine to watch them every morning. I like to entertain the thought that the numbers of their first catch could predict the amount of luck I have every day. They reel the boat out, and then lower a fish net. I wait. One, two, three seconds; they reel in a large catch. I smile to myself. Today is going to be a great day.

I lazily stroll down my narrow hallway, stopping for a moment—for just a moment—to gaze upon the burgundy, peeling wooden shelves cluttered with decades worth of strange items and treasures my father has been collecting. Often, I stop and simply gaze at the assortment of items. I can't help but imagine the history behind each and every one of them. The most recent item I identify is a small porcelain statue of an angel cradling a star. I've had it since 1975. Since I was three years old.

Strange statues depict pregnant women wrapped in Kente cloth with bowls over their heads. Some men, both young and old, are at work, and others are simple wooden carvings of Adinkra symbols.

Many other trinkets adorn the walls with origins unknown to my parents. One might even say that over time, these trinkets have become one with the house, their original owners now forgotten. Finally, I gaze at the game, Oware, my long-standing enemy. I simply can't wrap my head around the rules of arranging the stones into their compartments.

I rip my eyes away from the shelves and open the door that led outside. I am greeted with the sounds of early morning. The clucking of chickens, the barking of dogs, the stridulating of grasshoppers, and the lively chatter of the lady next door. I feel a sense of calm knowing that next week will be one of relaxation. A midterm break could have never come sooner. I get ready, wearing my favorite African-print jumpsuit and my best smile. I head out for the day.

As I walk through the streets, I twist and turn to avoid the many potholes in the ground. As I walk to the Tro-Tro station. I pass by the rundown store everyone calls the Bend Down Boutique. I'm not even sure if it ever had an actual name.

Many types of Ghanaian clothing are sprawled on the ground, from smocks to Kentes to Cabba and Slit and hand-woven purses and hats. Many beaded necklaces and bracelets lay on the table, collecting dust. I carefully select a beaded bracelet made of pink and purple beads. My mother always tells me that everything has a meaning, from how many frogs hop out of our gutters after heavy rain to how many times the  chickens cluck every morning. She would tell me, "The beads speak louder than words." I want to purchase one, but the shop is just as deserted as ever.

I wander the streets for a while. As the sun rises high into the sky, dozens of people emerge from their homes to start another day. Children squealing and chasing each other along the dusty paths; mothers and fathers getting ready for work; aunts and uncles gossiping under the large, shaded tree near the edge of town. I wander towards the chatter and later through the forest. I stumble onto the very same harbor that I see out of my window every day for years. The fishermen from this morning have returned to the chairs in front of their homes. They are in singlets, laughing and bellowing at jokes I can't make sense of. Their wives in Bubus happily chat as they cut fish, grill it, and pound Fufu. They take no notice of me. It is as if I were just another rock on the vast beach. I turn away.

I walk to the Tro-Tro station, my long-forgotten destination. It isn't the most fun place. People left and right and all around you, yell, plastic bottles clog the gutters, and sellers throng the front gates. The station air is thick with smoke and gas oil. I walk toward a car with a man hanging out of the door; he's calling for passengers to Kaneshie Market, my destination. I enter the Tro-Tro. It creaks as I enter. I take a seat in the second row from the door. The ceilings are lower than usual, and the window next to my seat has its curtain drawn. I pull out a slightly crumpled comic book from my jumpsuit's comically large pocket. It is *The Adventures of Tintin, Issue 20, Tintin in Tibet*. I've been looking for a place to be able to read this book. It seems that all the adults in my life have a personal vendetta against comics. Saying they're "too violent," "not real literature," or simply "it will rot my brain." I'm personally not sure why there seems to be this general negative consensus about comics in my area, but I always have to sneak around my parents and teachers if I want to read one, lest it gets confiscated.

The trip is short and bumpy, with the Tro-Tro's engine occasionally stopping in the middle of the trip. I exit and pay my fare. Already, I see hawkers selling all kinds of snacks, from Karkala to Adunle and Agblikaaklo. The Kaneshie market is a miasma of the senses. From the market, men and women are shouting to advertise their items to the crowded streets. There is an ever-lingering smell of skin musk, produce, and melting plastic. I make myself as small as possible as I squeeze through the crowded and narrow pathways.

Children younger than I are carelessly running around, bumping into everybody and anything. Across the road, boys are playing Chaskele, making quite the racket with the tins. But I went on as though I was deaf to the natural noisiness of the market.

I walk on, dodging street dogs and women with large metal baskets containing numerous items balanced over their heads. I am on a mission—it is a trivial one, but a mission, nonetheless. I walk on. Behind a large jewelry store that took up half the market stands a small stand with CDs. The covers are peeling, but they are legible enough to read. Picking up the CD labeled "Obra," I pay the kind old lady who owned the stand and walk back to the Tro-Tro parkingarea to head back. I gaze out the window during the Tro-Tro journey. The scene is nothing more than open farming land with a government school to break the monotony.

Many would say that it is a waste of time to make such a long journey for a simple CD, but I disagree. As I walk back home past the shops closing for the day, the chatter of the gossiping old ladies and the screaming of children cease. I feel a sense of tranquility wash over me. The only noise in the background was the pulling of burglar proof and the splashing of the waves on the shore. A call to the evening prayer followed by static is heard from the megaphone atop a Mosque.

I walk on, avoiding the potholes automatically and the Fanyogo cart passes by, the frog croaks. I arrive home, pull back the gate and shut it behind me. Chatter is heard from inside the house. I recognize the voices of my parents. I walk to my room, take my evening bath and put on pajamas and a bonnet.

I walk down the hallway, glancing at the shelves, this time only for a moment, before entering the living room. My mother and father are seated in their usual spots on the deep green couch. I greet them touching the tip of my head. They ask about my day, and I tell them about my trivial conquests, leaving out the part about Tintin. My mother's tired eyes gaze at me softly, and my father's cold eyes pierce my soul. We eat Kenkey and Tilapia for dinner. I do not like it, but I eat what I am given.

I load the CD into the player and watch as the box TV flickers to life in black and white. The audio starts off as static before becoming clear. I sit on the floor, and we watch the Obra in silence. It's a tradition that I have come to cherish. It's the little things that I love.

The Stereotypical Dutch

Isis Knols
Grade 8
Montessori Lyceum Rotterdam
Rotterdam, Holland

I woke up at 7 o'clock in the morning. I heard the cows moo in the distance and the rooster crowed cock-a-doodle. I walked over to the window, opened the curtains, and felt the calm breeze on my face. I looked outside and saw the windmills on the dike. From here, I was able to see the tulip fields. Maybe, after school, I and my friends could go for a lovely hike through the fields. Even though I enjoyed the view, it was time to put on my clothes.

I went downstairs to eat my breakfast. Every day, I eat one sandwich with cheese, one with hagelslag, an apple and, of course, drink a glass of milk. My mom had already prepared my lunch box filled with even more sandwiches. After breakfast, I put on my clumps, gave my mom a kiss, grabbed my backpack and headed over to my bike. I looked to my left and saw every child living on this dike do the exact same thing. It feels nice to fit in and be on time! I rode my bike on to the bike path and sped up, so that I could bike to school together with my friend Jolanda. A short fast sprint, because Jolanda only lives two mills further on the dike.

Jolanda's last name is Jansen. Her father is Johan Jansen. Her brother is Jan Jansen and her mother is Janneke Jansen. Everyone who lives on the dike is quite a stereotypical Dutch, but Jolanda's family surpasses everyone. They always look like a classic Dutch 1600s inspired tourist photo. Jolanda's braids always look perfect, her skirt has a nice dark blue colour, and her apron has a very floral print. Jolanda also always has fresh tulips in her bike's basket.

When I caught up with her, I greeted Jolanda, and she smiled back. I asked Jolanda, "Did you see the tulip fields this morning? Wouldn't it be lovely if after school, we hiked through the fields?"

"Didn't we do that yesterday? And the day before that?" she asked.

I was very confused. "Yes, so what!"

She looked down at the ground. "I just think that there maybe are other things to do."

'What is wrong with her' I thought.

I and Jolanda arrived at school. Our friends had already arrived and they walked over to us. "OMG!" said Saar. "Diederik looks so hot today with his new peasant scarf!"

"Wow I didn't even notice! Saar, you and Diederik would be a perfect match!"

"Diederik is wearing almost the exact same scarf as he did yesterday. What is the difference?" Jolanda asked.

Saar ignored Jolanda and kept talking, but I noticed Jolanda wasn't feeling very great today. We walked into the school building and into our first class. Jolanda was following a little behind.

The bell rang at 9:30. Dutch, German, Mathematics, and History were the first classes of the day. After those we had a small break. We sat in the square during the break as we talked about Diederik's scarf. I was getting bored. There were way more interesting things to do during break. We could jump rope or play hide and seek or just do something else rather than just listen to Saar going crazy about Diederik's scarf.

Jolanda was being very quiet so I asked her, "What would you like to do after school?"

She smiled at me and said, "How about we do something totally different! Like go to the movies and shop at the H&M or the Pull and Bear?" she sounded very excited.

I really tried my best to be a supportive friend, but neither of those things sounded anything Dutch or like Jolanda. "Uhm, wouldn't you enjoy helping your dad at the farm or going for a bike ride and eating poffertjes?" Her smile faded the moment I proposed my ideas.

"I'll just stay at home after school today." she said.

During our final lessons for the day, I couldn't stop thinking of Jolanda. I was feeling very worried about her. 'She sounded so different, so not Dutch. What could've happened?' After school, I was thinking so much about it that my mother proposed that I should do something with my hands. And there I was helping my dad with milking the cows.

He said, "You know Lieke, I once had a very similar experience as you."

I looked at my dad. "Really?"

He looked at me with a serious face and started telling his story. "The outside world has a specific way of looking at our country and we go along with that. But there are people who don't totally agree with that and love doing things that don't seem stereotypically Dutch. They are Dutch, but for the people living on the dike, they just don't seem to be Dutch. They respect us for living on this dike. We also respect them for living in big cities." Wow what did my dad just say? "I just mean that your ideas of a stereotypical Dutch person could be totally different from other's ideas."

I was still a little confused, but it felt like a new door had opened for me. I was also just very surprised that my dad could give me such good advice.

"Thank you, dad!" I said.

He smiled and nodded. I went back to our mill and told my mom about what dad had just told me. She also seemed quite confused, but we came up with a plan.

I rang the doorbell of Jolanda's mill. I was feeling very nervous. What if Jolanda thought of what I did as very weird, and she didn't find it helpful at all. Her mom opened the door. She looked very surprised at my little platter.

"It's very kind of you to do this for Jolanda" she said.

She let me in, and I walked upstairs to Jolanda's room. I opened the door and saw Jolanda standing in front of the mirror. She was wearing a blouse and a piece of clothing which, I think, they call jeans. She was also wearing weird clumps.

"They're called sneakers, Lieke. Nikes to be specific." She smirked as I looked up at her.

"I got you this. They're tickets for the movies, some foreign candies and this gift card for a store called Hollister?" She looked surprised but laughed and thanked me for all the gifts. I tried really hard to hide my real opinion about her outfit, but I was happy when my friend was happy.

Mystery in a Small Village

Lyly Antónia Cseh
Grade 11
Kairoly Mihali Bilingual Technical School
Budapaste, Hungary

Hi, I'm Eliza Gilbert. I live in Hungary, not far from Budapest, in a small village called Csomad. One day a very strange thing happened....

I was preparing for school one evening. I was watching Netflix while packing my bag. From my window, I saw a big light. I went outside to see what it was. It looked like an airplane, but it was flat like a plate. It lit up a house with a blue light. I knew who lived there because everyone in the village knew everyone. It was Aunt Zsuzsi's house. Her husband died last year, and she has been living alone in the big house ever since. She was nice to everyone. When I was little, she always used to invite me over and give me sweets. She used to tell me about World War II. She had interesting stories. In a flash, the blue light went out. And the object that looked like a plate disappeared as if it wasn't there. I thought I was dreaming, but I wasn't. My dog, Leo, started barking as soon as the plane disappeared. It was very strange. I went back to the house and tried to go to bed, but I couldn't sleep, and the unidentified object was all I could think about.

The next day I told my friends at school. They said that I must be crazy and that I must have been dreaming. They didn't believe me. On the way home, I got off the bus at Aunt Zsuzsi's house. There were a lot of police officers there. The whole house was surrounded with police tape. I went there and asked what was going on. A police officer told me that the old lady was missing. I said to myself, "Just after last night?" I didn't dare tell what I saw. They would have thought I was stupid. Later that night, when the police had gone, I returned to the house and climbed over the fence. Luckily for me, they left the front door open. Everything was in place as usual. It was cleaned out with no signs of abduction or a struggle. I heard a voice as if someone was in this house with me. I was very afraid. I saw a shadow, but it suddenly disappeared. I immediately ran out of the house. I started running home as fast as possible but felt that someone was following me. When I got to our house, I couldn't find my key. I heard him getting closer, but I didn't see anyone around me. I locked all the doors and windows. My parents didn't get home for another hour. When they finally entered the house, I almost hit them on the head with a wooden spoon (It was only means of defense that I could find). I didn't tell them anything. I went into my room and thought. Maybe ,Auntie Zsuzsi had been kidnapped by UFOs? I don't see why they'd want an old lady. Maybe, for her money? But I don't think they'd pay for Forint on Mars. Were they even aliens? They don't exist. That's how I fell asleep last night.

2 weeks later...

We still don't know anything about Aunt Zsuzsi. People disappear from the village from time to time. It's very scary. I was on my way home from school today and stopped at the local shop. Everybody was talking about strange disappearances. Auntie Zsuzsi was the first, but 2 more people had disappeared in 2 weeks. One was my former classmate Mark and another was his mother. The police officers were going around the village, knocking on every door, questioning people. They came to our house yesterday. I decided to tell them everything I knew. But all they said was: " This is a serious case, don't mess around, UFOs don't exist". My parents told me to stop being a policeman and investigating. That didn't stop me, I kept on looking into the case. 1 week later, strangely enough, Aunt Zsuzsi came back. She said she was in the hospital. But neither her grandchildren nor her children knew about it. She was acting very strangely. It was as if she had grown younger. I went to talk to her, but she didn't even recognize me. She couldn't tell me any stories, and she became very suspicious.

Gia's awesome trip to her roots

Sarah Susan Sony
Grade 8
Excelsior English School
Kottayam, Kerala, India

Gia is a girl who was born and brought up in the United States and had never once visited Kerala, even though it was her homeland. On a very special occasion, her mom decided to take her to Kerala for the first time.

"That was a very long trip, wasn't it?" said Gia with a tired look on her face.

"Yes," said her mom, "but we have plenty more to do, many people to meet, and many places to see, so you need to stay energized."

After completing all the immigration procedures and collecting their luggage at the airport, they went straight to the place where Gia's cousin Lyla and aunt were waiting for them. They got in the car and were happy to be together, as they usually only talked on FaceTime.

"This is the first time I am meeting you in person," said Gia.

"Yes, it is also very good that you came in the month of August," said Lyla.

"Why?" asked Gia, waiting for an answer.

"Well, August is the month of the harvest season, and we celebrate a festival well known in Kerala called Onam."

"Oh, Onam. I have only heard of it and know nothing else about it," said Gia, wishing she had known more than its name.

"Hey, no problem. I'd be very happy to tell you everything I know about it," said Lyla.

A smile came across Gia's face. "Okay, so let's begin with how the date of Onam is decided."

Onam is celebrated across communities in Kerala. The Onam celebration is based on the Panchangam, the Malayalam calendar, and

falls on the 22nd nakshatra, Thiruvonam, in the month of Chingam, which in the Gregorian calendar falls between August and September. It is celebrated over 10 days."

"10 days! That's so cool," said Gia with amazement.

"Yes, I know, and during these 10 days of celebration, students get holidays from schools to celebrate with their family and friends. The first day of Onam is called Atham. It is marked with the start of festivities at the Thrikkakara Vamanamoorthy Temple, Kochi. It is then followed by Chithira, Chodi, Vishakam, Anizham, Thriketta, Moolam, Pooradam, Uthradom, and Thriruvonam. Thiruvonam is the most auspicious day as it marks the end of the Onam celebration." Said Lyla.

"So then will we be able to celebrate Onam since it's in August?" asked Gia.

"Yes, we can, although Onam started a week ago, we've still got 3 more days left to enjoy and eat a wonderful grand feast called Onasadhya," said Lyla.

"Onasadhya? What is that?" asked Gia.

"Onasadhya is where we have rice, sambar, parippu curry, ghee, pappadam, avial, different thorns, and many more vegetable delicacies, and we get to eat it all on a banana leaf; in the end, we get to eat a dessert called payasam; it is super delicious," said Lyla.

"That's great; I won't miss the food at least," said Gia laughingly.

Also, since you just came to Kerala, there is one awesome thing happening today that I don't think you have ever seen before, said Lyla with excitement.

"What is it?" asked Gia with curiosity.

"The Nehru Trophy Boat Race is happening today, in Punnamada Lake, Alappuzha, and guess what, we are almost there," said Lyla.

"We are?" asked Gia.

"Yes," said Lyla with enthusiasm. After a few minutes they had reached the spot. "Okay, it will start in an hour or so as everyone has to come, so in the meantime, shall I tell you about this amazing race held every year?"

"Yes, of course, I am eagerly waiting," said Gia.

"Okay, so the Nehru Trophy Boat Race is amongst the premier snake boat races in Kerala. It is held on the second Saturday of August every year and draws in a massive crowd. People gather in large numbers to watch nearly 100 ft long boats compete against each other to the tune of old boat songs on both sides of the lake. Punnamada Lake is the location for the race where the contestants' line up to battle it out. It's such an exciting experience to watch how all the teams compete. Did you also know that there is a story behind how the Nehru Trophy Boat Race got its name?" said Lyla.

"There is?" Can you tell me about it? asked Gia.

"Yes, of course, so the story behind this water regatta getting its name goes back to the visit of Pandit Jawaharlal Nehru, the first Prime Minister of India, in 1952. He was so enchanted by the sight of the majestic snake boats that he leapt onto one of the snake boats himself, ignoring his security cover. Later in the year, he would donate a silver trophy in the form of a snake boat as a gift for the memories of the time he spent there. Hence the race would later go on to be named the Nehru Trophy Boat Race." said Lyla.

"That is such a beautiful story," said Gia.

"It is also during this season that the area comes to life with ceremonial water processions and beautiful water floats. From the huge 'Chundan Valloms' (snake boats) to small country rafts, the waters are under the control of the expert oarsmen who put on a show that one can never forget. It is a form of art in itself," said Lyla.

"Look! It's starting, said Gia with joy.

"Just in time," said Lyla. They saw how each team rowed through the dark green lake singing old boat songs with great vigor and team spirit. Each team did their very best and made it through the finish line. The team that had won was awarded the Nehru Trophy. After everything was over, Gia and Lyla reached home.

"That was such an amazing day! Even though it is my first day here, I must tell my friends in the States about the amazing time here and about Onam and the boat races that happen here in Kerala every year. I knew Kerala was rich in culture and traditions, but I did not know it would be this fun and awesome. I have never seen anything like this as we have seen today," said Gia.

"There is more to see and to learn about Kerala. This is just the beginning," said Lyla with a smile.

Kalpeni Band

Isna Bathool
Grade 8
Government Senior Basic school
House Kalpeni Island, Lakshadweep,
UT of India.

Imagine a magical place far, far away, surrounded by sparkling blue seas and tiny islands covered in soft white sand. That's Lakshadweep!

It's like a secret treasure hidden in the middle of the ocean. Kalpeni is one of the islands in Lakshadweep, inhabited as an atoll in the Union Territory of India. I live in Kalpeni.

Life in Lakshadweep is peaceful and happy. Families live in small villages where everyone knows each other and helps one another like one big family. They celebrate special occasions with music, dancing, and delicious feasts of fresh seafood caught from the sea.

Many students in Lakshadweep live in small villages scattered across the islands. Their daily commute to school is a scenic journey by boat or walking along sandy paths lined with coconut palms.

The story I want to tell is about how I joined the band team in Kalpeni and how that experience motivated me. One day when I came home from school, a few children and a teacher named Najmuddin were standing in the schoolyard. When I was passing the school gate, the teacher called my name and came to me. He said that these were NCC students and asked me to join them.

The teacher said, "You have the ability to join."

At that moment, I didn't realize my potential, but later I decided to join the NCC.

As an NCC cadet, I practiced in parades for the first month. Later, I was promoted to the band team. We didn't have a trained bandmaster at that time. But due to the great initiative of Najmuddin Sir, we got a bandmaster.

So, as the bandmaster hails from Kerala, the rhythms had taken on a new flavor. We both speak Malayalam, but there was a slight variation between our languages. Most of the Lakshadweep islanders communicate in Malayalam, while Mahi (or Mahl), a language similar to old Sinhalese, is spoken on Minicoy. Additionally, some residents are proficient in Hindi.

Within a month of his training, we got an opportunity to present our band in the Republic Day parade at New Delhi. It was a happy moment for all of us!

I have been on drum duty for the past few months. I have been promoted to the position of band leader. During these days, it was our band team that received many of the admin officers arriving at Kalpani. All these were our practicing sessions just before the Delhi journey.

All the officials and visitors enjoyed their life here because our land is very beautiful and the Dweep life is so peaceful.

Lakshadweep is special because it's home to so many amazing things. First, picture the sea around the islands. It's so clear and shiny, like a giant mirror reflecting the bright sun and fluffy clouds. You can see colorful fish swimming happily in the water and beautiful corals growing on the rocks beneath.

On the islands themselves, there are coconut trees everywhere! Their tall, swaying branches provide shade from the hot sun, and their sweet fruits are delicious to eat. People in Lakshadweep use coconuts for everything, from making tasty food to crafting useful things like baskets and mats.

But it's not just about fun and games in Lakshadweep. People there take care of these beautiful islands and the creatures that live there. They use clean energy from the sun and the wind, and they make sure to keep their beaches and seas clean and free from trash.

Sometimes, the islands face big storms called cyclones, but the brave people of Lakshadweep work together to keep each other safe and rebuild their homes afterward. The population is primarily concentrated on the islands of Andrott, Kavaratti, Minicoy, and Amini.

As we were leaving for Delhi from Agati airport, we received surprising news... We got an offer to meet our honorable prime minister! When we flew from the Agatti airport to Delhi via Bangalore, my mind was flying before me. When my eyes were watching the beauty of my land, my mind was visualizing the Republic Day parade.

It's a magical place where nature's beauty and people's kindness come together to create a wonderful paradise in the middle of the ocean. In Lakshadweep, every day feels like an adventure, with new things to discover and explore. The same thing is happening in my mind now.

As a Dweep student, this is my proud moment. I got this opportunity because of my band performance. After my school life, I will learn music and will form a music band in Kalpeni. I hope that the Kalpeni band gets opportunities to perform all over the Indian cities.

As the final chords of our latest performance fade into the night, as a member of the Kalpeni band, I feel a glance of hope in my heart. I feel closer to my dreams of sharing our music with audiences far and wide.

The days are coming when the Kalpeni band will receive invitations to perform in cities across India, from the bustling streets of Mumbai to the vibrant culture of Kolkata.

With each performance, we will bring a piece of our island home to new audiences, spreading joy and inspiration with every melody we play. And as we travel from city to city, we will never forget the humble beginnings that brought us together—the shared love of music and the bonds of friendship that have grown stronger with each passing day.

Yes, the days are coming for the Kalpeni band, and we will seize every opportunity that comes our way, knowing that our music has the power to unite, uplift, and inspire all who hear it.

And so, with hearts full of hope and determination, I set out on my journey, ready to conquer the world with the songs at the same time.

A Transcontinental Friendship

Moumita Ghosh
Grade 11
Sarsuna Girls High School
Kolkata, West Bengal, India

My name is Sikha. I am a Bengali girl living in Kolkata. When my father was working, we lived in Dubai, and I completed my entire schooling there. I would like to share an amazing experience of a transcontinental friendship that was once lost but reunited after a long time.

While living in Dubai, I met a Canadian girl who studied in my school. Her name was Liza, and we became close friends within a few days. Shortly after, Liza and her family moved back to Canada due to personal reasons. I felt very sad when she left. Within a year, I also returned to India after my father's retirement and started living in Kolkata.

I always remembered Liza, my best friend, whom I had not met or spoken to since she left Dubai. I often searched for her on social media. One morning, I suddenly received a notification on my phone through Facebook. When I checked, it was none other than Liza, my best friend. I was overjoyed. We talked extensively on Facebook and became best friends like before. We used to share and confide in each other about everything.

A few months later, I invited her to my brother's wedding. She was always fascinated by the Indian festivals and traditions, so she readily agreed to come to India at my request, but she had one condition: she would also like to visit the Durga Puja pandel before she returns.

Durga Puja is the biggest puja in West Bengal. My brother's marriage was in August, and Durga Puja was in October. I told her that if she wanted to see Durga Puja, then she must stay at my house for 2 more months after my brother's marriage. She was a bit hesitant to stay for such a long period, but later she agreed. I was very excited as we would meet again after so many years. Her parents sent her alone to India with my faith, and I picked her up at the airport. She was very happy to see me. Then I took her to my house, which is in Behala, south Kolkata.

Liza was very excited because she had never seen a Bengali wedding before. Finally, the wedding day arrived. The whole house was decorated with lights, panels, a variety of flowers, etc. The first ritual that she attended was "gaye holud.". This ritual is very popular and fun among Bengalis. The ceremony involves applying turmeric paste on the skin of the bride and groom to give them a radiant glow. Family and friends gather to sing traditional songs and apply turmeric paste to the couple. Liza thoroughly enjoyed the 'gaye holud' ceremony. And then we came back home to dress up for the evening ceremony.

Liza and I dressed up in Bengali sarees with a bun at the back, loaded with Rojonigondha flowers (tuberose flowers). We also wore golden ornaments, which gave us a perfect look for a Bengali wedding ceremony. Liza had never worn a saree before, but that day she wore her first saree, and she was very happy. She danced and sang a lot with my family, and we all had lots of fun together.

We all got ready as soon as the 'Gaye holud' ritual was over and reached the bride's house, where we got a warm welcome. The main wedding ceremony took place under a beautifully decorated mandap, where the bride and groom exchanged garlands and took the sacred vows. The traditional bridal attire for a Bengali bride is the stunning red and white saree, known as the "Banarasi" saree. She was adorned with gold jewelry, including a heavy necklace, earrings, bangles, and anklets. The bride's forehead was decorated with a red and white bindi, and her hair was adorned with flowers or ornamental hairpins. And my brother, in typical bridegroom style, wore a white dhoti and kurta, paired with a silk or cotton Panjabi. He also had a 'topor' (traditional Bengali wedding turban) and a garland of flowers.

I explained all the wedding rules to Liza, and she enjoyed them as she had never seen such a wedding before. All the cousins and Liza danced a lot together and had a lot of fun. After the wedding was over, we were left with one more major ritual, which generally happens one day after the wedding, known as "Bou Bhaat.". On this day, officially, the bride takes charge of the house.

After the wedding, we had lots of fun over the next month and a half, and Durga Puja time had begun. So, on the occasion of Durga Puja, Liza and I did a lot of shopping together. Durga Puja celebrations in Kolkata begin with 'Mahalaya.'. Mahalaya, which occurs seven days before Durga Puja, signals the arrival of Durga, the goddess of supreme power. It serves as an invocation or invitation for the mother goddess to descend to Earth. This invitation is extended through the recitation of sacred mantras.

Durga Puja is an old tradition of Hinduism. Its exact origins are unclear, but the surviving manuscripts from the 14th century provide guidelines for Durga Puja. Although it is a celebration of the Hindu sect, people of other religions are also a part of this celebration in various ways. That is, Durga Puja is not just a ritual of a religion or a community; it's a celebration of Bangali's traditional inclusivity.

Mahalaya is observed with reverence and nostalgia. It is a time when people wake up before dawn to listen to the mesmerizing recitation of "Mahisasura Mardini" from the ancient scripture "Chandi Path" broadcast on the radio. This invocation narrates the story of Goddess Durga descending to earth to defeat Mahishasura, symbolizing the victory of good over evil.

On the day of Mahalaya, at 5 am, I woke up Liza, and we all listened to Mahalaya together. On Mahalaya day everyone wakes up at 5 am and listens to Mahalaya with family. Durga Puja came a few days after Mahalaya. Durga Puja preparations are in high gear after

Mahalaya. Artisans and sculptors work tirelessly to create magnificent idols of Goddess Durga and her divine angels.

The streets of the city come alive with the sound of artisans making idols out of clay, a process that requires skill, precision, and devotion. Simultaneously, pandals, temporary structures to house idols, started cropping up across the city.

The festival's most significant period spans the final five days when various rituals and 'pujas' are conducted in elaborately decorated structures called pandals. These panels are often larger and more ornate than simple altars or porches. It serves as a temporary home for the idols of Goddess Durga and other deities. Each panel is a work of art, with a specific theme or design and furnished as per concept. Some panels draw inspiration from mythology, while others reflect contemporary social issues or artistic innovation. Competition for the most creative panel is fierce, with neighborhoods and communities competing to outdo each other in grand this.

We traveled a lot and had a lot of fun. Liza tasted many kinds of food that are very popular among us Bengalis. Like 'Papdi chat,' 'Bhelpuri, Fuchka, ghugni chat, rasgulla, dahivada, etc. Liza had never tried Bengali food before. She liked their popular dishes very much. We used to visit new places every day. The main Bengali Durga Puja is 4 days long, and the 5th day, which we know as "Bijaya Dashami,".

On Liza's turn to go back to her home country, we all felt sad because Liza had become like one of our family members. I used to think of her as my own sister. I went to drop Liza at the airport. We couldn't stop our tears from flowing as we would miss each other. Liza promised me that she'll be back soon and also invited me to Canada. This put a smile on our faces, and we gave each other a tight hug.

I am sure I will meet Liza again, either in India, as Liza grew very fond of our culture, or in Canada, where she invited me to go and stay with her during Christmas time. I'm looking forward to meeting with my childhood friend again and reliving all the memories we created together.

Masterpiece

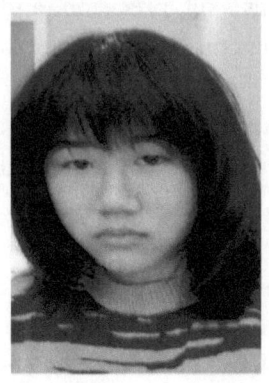

Helena Katherine Chandra
Grade 10
Binus School Simprug
Jakarta, Indonesia

No! It can't be like this!" shouted Mas Agung, an artist. "My designs have to be as good as possible," he said, "until I can create works that shock the art world throughout Indonesia. I can't stop now."

Mas Agung constantly pulled out blank canvases, paints, and paper from a large teakwood cupboard overflowing with traditional art tools— canting pens, wax, and natural dyes—while tossing aside used papers and failed sketches he deemed useless. As a finalist in a prestigious national batik-pattern-making competition held in Solo, he was determined to invent the most extraordinary patterns inspired by Javanese mythology, the lush landscapes of Sumatra, and the intricate flora of Kalimantan, all to achieve a dream he had carried since childhood.

"Stop it," said his wife, adjusting her faded kebaya as she watched him obsessively sketch. "Just stop. You'll tire yourself out. It's been hours."

But Mas Agung was too focused on his work to even register her concern. He gripped his pencil tightly and sat at the low wooden table, never breaking his intense gaze from a seemingly plain piece of paper. Having failed multiple competitions—from Bali to Bandung—he kept trying, believing this could be the moment his name would echo beyond his village.

"You said you wanted to be a well-known artist," his wife reminded him softly.

"Yes, that's why I'm doing this," Mas Agung grumbled. "I keep failing! But I know if I try hard enough, people will finally see my art and designs for what they are. This nation will see me. Everyone will."

As they argued, failed sketches rained down around them, building up in a growing pile near the woven bamboo mat. His wife knelt beside it and quietly began uncrumpling a few sheets.

She sat still, flipping through more discarded designs—patterns echoing the curves of Toraja carvings, the waves of Bali's southern coast, and the earthy tones of Papuan tribal art.

"What are you doing?" Mas Agung asked, still immersed in a fresh sketch.

"...These are good, don't you know that?" she whispered.

"Huh? No, I don't see it. They're all failed sketches," he replied.

"These are good! Good! And you can't see that!" she cried. "I would wear batik with patterns like these—they're beautiful! They speak of places and stories across our islands!"

Mas Agung paused, pencil hovering. His strokes, once frantic, slowed.

"You... Huh?" He stammered, eyes finally meeting hers.

"Yes! I told you," she said firmly. "I don't know why, but you don't see the worth in them." She tossed the sketches back to him.

"But if they're that nice, then..." He murmured, "...why didn't they win—"

"Because they don't have to!" she interrupted. "Even if you don't win, even if the judges don't get it, there are still people like me who truly love what you've made!"

Mas Agung finally looked down at his current drawing -a rhythmic pattern inspired by the waves crashing along Sulawesi's rugged shores.

His wife stepped closer, eyes soft.

"I don't know what you're doing this for, Mas, but you can't destroy yourself over it," she said. "And no one's bothered to tell you this, but... you've been great all along."

He sighed. And without a word, he put the pencil down.

School trip

Malika Ahmed
Grade 7
Al-Meeqat School
Al-Najaf, Iraq

As usual, on my way home from school, I was exhausted while my friends talked about the educational trip planned for tomorrow. I was not eager to go on the trip, as they decided to visit one of the monuments in Iraq in the city of Babylon.

Our teacher mentioned that we would visit one of the Seven Wonders. I was skeptical. How could there be traces from thousands of years ago still described as one of the Seven Wonders? Especially since we live in a world of technology and wonders. But I had no choice but to go, as it was part of my school duties.

The next morning, I saw my mother preparing the luggage for the trip, and she was happy. When I asked about her happiness, she said this was a good opportunity to learn about ancient civilizations and discover one of the Seven Wonders. She mentioned the next trip would be with the family to Egypt to see the pyramids. Her words did not increase my enthusiasm, so I still had to go to Babylon to complete the history assignment.

I went to school and joined the trip. The sky was clear, and the sun shone beautifully. When we arrived, I got off the bus and stood before the gates of the old city. A shiver ran through my body as I saw a gorgeous artistic painting with high walls and ancient temples.

The enthusiasm for exploration began to increase more and more to discover every corner of the city to learn about the ancient history of Babylon. There I met a tour guide, and he began to explain about the Babylonian civilization, as it is considered one of the most important ancient civilizations that influenced the development of humanity. The history of Babylon dates to the third millennium BC.

I continued walking around by myself, as I was amazed by the infrastructure surrounding the city. I started writing some of the symbols on the walls, as the first symbols used for reading and writing were called the Akkadian language, which is one of the first written languages in human history. Then I saw the view of the famous Hanging Gardens, which is considered one of the Seven Wonders of the Ancient World.

When I arrived home, I told my mother how enjoyable and useful the trip was, and I was ready for the next trip with the family to Egypt, where the pyramids are located. I understood the necessity of educational trips and travel in an individual's life, as it opens the doors to understanding and learning about new cultures and ancient and exciting history.

Deirdre's Destiny

Aadya Krithika Santosh
Grade 9
Adamstown Community College
Dublin, Ireland.

More than a thousand years ago in Ireland, there was a man named Malcolm Harper, a kind-hearted man with a wife, a house, and lands to his name, but no children. One day, a seer passing by was overcome by a disturbing prophecy: Malcolm's future daughter would bring turmoil and tragedy to many in Ireland. This ominous foretelling spoke of much bloodshed and the demise of three valiant heroes due to his daughter.

Soon enough, Malcolm and his wife welcomed a daughter, whom they named Deirdre. Fearing the prophecy would come true, they hid Deirdre away from the world and men with a willing foster mother in a small, concealed house in a mound of earth at the edge of a woods.

Several years passed, and Deirdre grew to become a beautiful young lady, with gorgeous eyes and long, shiny hair. Under her foster mother's guidance, she had acquired several skills fit for a noble lady of that time. One windy night, an exhausted and lost hunter stumbled upon the mound, seeking refuge to rest.

As he lay down, he heard Deirdre playing music and thought she was a fairy. He shouted, "Let me in! I am a hunter, lost and cold. Please provide me with warmth and shelter." Hearing his pleas for help, Deirdre's compassionate nature led her to open the door to the stranger, despite her foster mother's warnings. Little did she know, this act of kindness would set the sinister prophecy into motion.

Upon encountering Deirdre, the hunter was in awe of her unparalleled beauty and saw an opportunity to fulfill his own wishes. Since many lords were looking for a wife, the hunter knew that by bringing her to the attention of King Connachar and his court, he would be rewarded greatly. Ignoring Deirdre's foster mother's request for secrecy, the hunter told about her existence to the king, who immediately set out to take her as his wife. Although she was hesitant at first, she agreed she would marry Connachar, as long as he gave her a year and a day's delay before the wedding. Happy with her terms, Connachar took her back to his palace, where every wish of hers would be taken care of by her ladies-in-waiting.

Once, when walking with her ladies, Deirdre encountered Naois, a renowned hero, and his brothers, and found herself falling in love with the young lord. Abruptly, gathering her courage and leaving her ladies behind, she ran after him and asked, "Naois, son of Uisnech, will you leave me behind?" Naois, turning back to respond to the calls, found himself smitten by Deirdre. Unable to resist their feelings, Deirdre fled with Naois and his brothers to Scotland, where they lived in peace until the looming date of Deirdre's promised marriage to Connachar came closer.

Connachar, determined to reclaim Deirdre, devised a cunning plan to ensnare Naois and his brothers. Connachar sent his uncle, Ferchar Mac Ro, and his 3 sons to accompany them from Scotland. Deirdre, having had a dream foreseeing the impending danger, pleaded with Naois not to go. Realizing the political checkmate Connachar had backed them in, Naois realized that they had no choice but to go, lest they face the King's wrath. Ferchar, having come to the same conclusion too, vowed that he and his three sons would stand by Deirdre, Naois, and his brothers' side. Soon, they returned to Connachar's court, where they were met with hostility. A fearsome battle ensued, with Ferchar's sons valiantly defending Naois and Deirdre against Connachar's forces.

Desperate to thwart their escape, Connachar enlisted the help of a powerful magician, who conjured obstacles to impede their escape across the loch. Despite these magical hindrances, Naois and his brothers pressed onward, enduring trials of forest, sea, and finally ice.

Tragically, their journey ended in misery, with Naois and his brothers succumbing to the magician's poisonous ice. Connachar, unable to find Deirdre, desperately asked the magician to part the sea, only to find Deirdre weeping inconsolably next to the bodies of her love and his brothers. Carrying the bodies back to shore, Connachar ordered his men to dig graves for the three brothers. Eventually, when the graves were finally big enough, in grief and despair, Deirdre chose to join her beloved Naois in death, rather than face a future without him.

Angered by her act and fueled by his spite against Naois, Connachar ordered his men to bury Deirdre on the opposite side of the loch instead of with her love. As they lay in rest forevermore on opposite sides of the loch, two fir trees grew from their graves. As time passed, the trees ended up entwining with each other. Though Connachar cut down the merging branches every time they grew, the love between Naois and Deirdre persisted as the branches grew anew. Eventually, even Connachar acknowledged the futility of trying to erase their love, allowing nature to take its course and honoring their memory in peaceful rest.

Throughout history, Deirdre's story has come to mean many things. In the early twentieth century, Irish poets Yeats and Synge used Deirdre's story to symbolize Irish oppression. The characters, Deirdre, the young, innocent beauty; Naois, her love; and Connachar, the powerful and greedy king who hunted her down, reflected the political climate then. Deirdre represented the Irish, and Naois, their beliefs, as they were oppressed by the kingdom of England, like Connachar.

However, recently Deirdre's story has come to stand for human rights advocacy. It talks about marginalized communities, like Deirdre, when standing for their values, like when she helped the hunter even against warnings because of her kindness; they were persecuted and aren't given basic rights by people like Connachar.

Nevertheless, Deirdre's story is not only powerful in the injustice it portrays but also in its simpler message—love. Even when facing several adversities, Deirdre and Naois' love persevered, illustrating that above anything else, the bonds we have with our loved ones are the strongest.

The City of Treasures

Carlo Maria Cascone
Grade 9
High school for Foreign Languages
Salerno, Italy

Once upon a time in the enchanting city of Rome, ancient ruins basked in a warm golden glow. Bustling streets were filled with locals and tourists, each immersed in the rich history and vibrant energy that permeated the air.

In the city's heart, a young archaeologist named Mia embarked on a thrilling quest. She had dedicated her life to uncovering Rome's hidden secrets and preserving its cultural heritage. Mia's passion for archaeology was ignited during childhood visits to the Colosseum, where she marveled at the ancient structure's grandeur.

One fateful morning, Mia received a cryptic letter from an anonymous sender. The letter spoke of a long-lost artifact, rumored to possess mystical powers, buried deep beneath Rome's cobblestone streets. Intrigued and filled with adventure, Mia decided to begin her most daring excavation yet.

Equipped with her trusty tools and accompanied by her loyal canine companion, Max, Mia set out on her quest. She began her investigation at the Capitoline Museums, poring over ancient manuscripts and consulting renowned archaeologists. Piece by piece, she unraveled the clues hidden within the city's historical archives.

Mia's journey took her to the Roman Forum, where she discovered an ancient inscription carved into a weathered stone. It revealed a hidden passage leading to an underground labyrinth beneath the city. With curiosity fueling her determination, Mia descended into the depths, her heart pounding with anticipation.

The labyrinth proved to be a treacherous maze of winding tunnels and secret chambers. Mia encountered puzzles and traps that tested her intellect and courage. She deciphered ancient riddles, studied intricate carvings on the walls, and navigated through darkness with only a flickering torch to guide her way.

As she ventured deeper into the labyrinth, Mia encountered remnants of past civilizations. She uncovered pottery fragments, ancient coins, and long-forgotten artifacts. Each discovery filled her with a sense of awe and reverence, connecting her to the lives and stories of those who had walked the same paths centuries ago.

After days of relentless exploration, Mia reached a vast chamber bathed in an ethereal glow. The room was adorned with magnificent statues and intricately carved pillars. In the center, atop a pedestal, lay the object of her search—a gleaming, jewel-encrusted amulet.

With trembling hands, Mia reached out and lifted the amulet from its resting place. Its presence radiated a tangible energy, filling the chamber with an otherworldly aura. Mia sensed that she had stumbled upon something truly extraordinary.

The amulet was said to possess the power to heal wounds and bring harmony to those who possessed it. Mia knew that such power must be treated with utmost care and respect. She vowed to use it for the greater good and to protect it from falling into the wrong hands.

As Mia emerged from the labyrinth, she was met with a newfound sense of purpose and responsibility. She shared her discovery with the local authorities and scholars, ensuring the artifact would be protected and studied for generations to come. The news of her remarkable journey spread throughout the city, inspiring others to explore their own passions and uncover the hidden treasures of Rome.

Mia's adventure in Rome propelled her into the spotlight of the archaeological community. She was invited to deliver lectures at prestigious universities and museums, sharing her knowledge and experiences with eager audiences. Her expertise and dedication earned her a prominent role in the excavations across the city, and she became a respected figure in the field of archaeology.

Recognizing the importance of preserving Rome's cultural heritage, Mia established a foundation dedicated to funding archaeological research and restoration projects. She worked tirelessly to ensure that ancient sites were protected and that the stories of Rome's past were celebrated and shared with the world.

Over the years, Mia's legacy grew, and her name became synonymous with adventure and discovery. She mentored aspiring archaeologists, passing on her wisdom and passion to the next generation. Her foundation flourished, funding groundbreaking research and contributing to the preservation of Rome's historical treasures.

As she walked the streets of Rome, Mia knew that every stone held a story waiting to be uncovered. She reveled in the city's rich tapestry of history, forever captivated by its magic. Her unwavering dedication and love for archaeology ensured that Rome's treasures would continue to be unearthed and celebrated for generations to come.

And so, the tale of Mia, the intrepid archaeologist, became etched into the tapestry of Rome's history, reminding us of all the enduring power of curiosity, discovery, and the indomitable spirit of adventure. While the amulet she discovered held immense power, it was Mia.

Unravelling Japan's Mysteries: Kaori's Story of Courage

Kaito
Grade 6
Sakado Elementary School
Saitama, Japan

In the heart of Tokyo, where neon lights pulsed like electric veins and ancient shrines stood in quiet defiance of modernity, there existed a peculiar antique shop hidden in a narrow alleyway. The store, known as 'Mystic Relics', bore no signboard, only a faded noren[1] swaying gently in the night breeze. Few knew of its existence, and even fewer dared to enter.

Mystic Relics was owned by Hideo; an enigmatic elderly man whose eyes carried the weight of centuries. Rumors whispered that his artifacts held mystical powers, remnants of Japan's forgotten past. Unlike the city's bustling merchants, Hideo was selective, allowing only those deemed worthy to glimpse his most treasured relics—objects bound by ancient curses and blessings alike.

One stormy evening, the rain poured down in relentless sheets, and a young girl named Kaori stumbled into the shop seeking shelter. A middle school student with insatiable curiosity, she was immediately drawn to the dimly lit interior, where the scent of incense and aged parchment filled the air.

Hideo, peering over his round spectacles, studied the drenched visitor with quiet amusement. "You are not here by accident," he murmured, gesturing for her to step forward.

Behind the main room lay a hidden chamber, its entrance concealed behind an ornate folding screen adorned with delicate paintings of

---

1. *Noren* (暖簾): *Traditional Japanese fabric dividers hung between rooms, on walls, in doorways, or in windows.*

cranes and cherry blossoms. Inside, the flickering glow of paper lanterns revealed relics from all corners of Japan: an elegantly crafted katana with a tsuka[2] wrapped in silk, a rusted tsuba[3] inscribed with forgotten kanji[4], a tea ceremony set bearing the insignia of a feudal lord, and among them, a tarnished wooden chest carved with mythical creatures *(dragons, kitsune, and tengu)* whispering tales of old through their intricate designs.

Hideo traced a gnarled finger over the engravings. "This belonged to the samurai Takeda no Kenshiro, who, centuries ago, sought the path to immortality. Within this chest lies a map to a hidden woodland, said to hold the wisdom of the ancients."

The legend spoke of a sacred forest lost to time. But Kaori was not the only one drawn to this mystery. Shadowy figures had long sought the chest, believing its secrets could grant them dominion over fate itself.

Determined to uncover the truth, Kaori embarked on a journey through Tokyo's hidden past. She deciphered riddles in old poetry, followed clues inscribed on forgotten shrines, and slipped through the underground pathways once used by spies. Along the way, she

---

2. *Tsuka (柄): The hilt or handle of a Japanese sword.*
3. *Tsuba (鍔, or 鐔): A flat iron plate that separates the hilt of the sword from the blade and protects the hand of the sword wielder.*
4. *Kanji: A type of Japanese writing system, based on symbols which represent words or ideas.*

encountered strange obstacles—like an old trickster who led her astray and eerie whispers from a long-abandoned temple.

With every challenge, Kaori unraveled more than just the samurai's secret; she uncovered pieces of Japan's past, its forgotten tales and hidden wisdom.

At last, Kaori reached the final trial: a riddle left by Takeda himself. As she recited an ancient poem inscribed on the chest, the lock unlatched. But instead of revealing a conventional treasure, the map transformed into a swirl, vanishing into the night air.

Hideo, who had silently followed her journey, smiled. "The true treasure was never the forest, but the wisdom you gained. Knowledge is the path to eternity."

With newfound understanding and an unquenchable thirst for adventure, Kaori bid farewell to Hideo and the mystic relics, knowing

that Tokyo's labyrinthine streets still held untold stories waiting to be discovered. And so, as the lanterns dimmed and the rain ceased, she stepped out into the city, ready to chase the mysteries of Japan once more.

The Desert Rose: A Story of the Enchanting Jordan

Rama Ahmad
Grade 7
Al Hassad Al Tarbawy
Amman, Jordan

A young girl named Layla lived in the center of Jordan, between golden dunes and ancient ruins. She resided in a small village tucked away amid the steep mountains of Petra. Petra is a historic and archaeological city in southern Jordan, famous for its rock-cut architecture and water conduit system. Often called the "Rose City" because of the color of the sandstone from which it is carved, Petra was bordered by olive groves that whispered stories of generations past.

Layla stood apart from other young women in her town. While her contemporaries were content with the comfortable settings of their homes, she craved the excitement and discovery found in the world. The desert winds that blew across the vast landscapes of her nation made her spirit as free as those winds themselves.

Layla's eyes would light up with awe and fascination during her adventures. As she made her way through the winding village alleys, she would pause to listen to birds singing and wind rustling through leaves. The desert, however, was her most beloved destination.

Layla felt a unique and powerful connection to the desert. A wave of astonishment washed over her as she absorbed the stunning view of golden sands and majestic dunes surrounding her. She would spend hours traveling through shifting landscapes, marveling at desert flowers that flourished in the harshest conditions and delighting in the soft sand beneath her feet. During Layla's exploration in the desert, she happened to find a secret oasis along the way. The oasis appeared to be a mirage in the middle of the desert; it was a shimmering body of water that was encircled by tall palm trees and colorful flowers. It was a place that was unspoiled by the rest of the world; it was a place of peace and calm.

While Layla was sitting by the edge of the oasis, she picked out a single rose that was growing in the sand. The aroma of its petals, which were a deep shade of scarlet, filled the air with a sweetness that overwhelmed the senses. There was nothing so stunning that Layla had ever witnessed. Layla was so adamant about safeguarding the desert rose that she decided to construct a modest shelter around it. Her daily routine consisted of going to the oasis, where she would water the rose and attend to its requirements. As a result, the desert rose would blossom in a manner that was more radiant and stunning than it had ever been before.

As the news of Layla's oasis spread across the hamlet, people from all over the place began to make their way there to witness the magical desert transformation. They were awestruck by its appearance and shared stories of Layla's generosity and passion for the cause. Despite the passage of time and Layla's maturation, her profound affection for the desert remained unshaken. As she proceeded to explore its immense breadth, she came across centuries-old mysteries and hidden treasures along the way. Even though she finally left her community to go to other parts of the world, she would never forget the desert rose that she had seen.

Specifically, Layla had gained the knowledge that beauty may be discovered in the most unanticipated of locations and that there are times when the most valuable riches are concealed in the most improbable of locations. As a result, the tale of Layla and the desert rose became a legend, serving as a tribute to the eternal charm of Jordan's landscapes as well as the limitless depths of the human soul. Layla's spirit continued to live on in the hearts of those who knew her, serving as a beacon of hope and inspiration for future generations.

Harmonical Landscapes of the Kazakh Steppe

Asanova Sevinch
Grade 9
Nazarbayev Intellectual School of
Chemical and Biological Directions
Shymkent, Kazakhstan

Amid the vast landscapes of Kazakhstan, where golden steppes stretch as far as the eye can see, a tale unfolds that weave together the tapestry of its rich culture. In the small village of Nur-Sultan, nestled beneath the shadow of the Altai Mountains, lived two friends, Aisha and Nurzhan, who embarked on a journey to explore the depths of their homeland's cultural heritage.

Their adventure began in the heart of Almaty, where the bustling bazaars overflowed with vibrant colors and the tantalizing aroma of spices filled the air. Aisha and Nurzhan navigated through the labyrinth of stalls, immersing themselves in the diversity of Kazakh textiles and handcrafted treasures. They marveled at the intricate patterns that told stories of nomadic traditions passed down through generations.

Leaving the city's vibrant pulse behind, the friends ventured into the timeless steppes. Along the way, they stumbled upon a nomad's yurt, where an elder named Bakyt welcomed them with open arms. Around the flickering fire, Bakyt shared tales of the Kazakh nomadic way of life, emphasizing the deep connection between the people and the land.

Invigorated by Bakyt's stories, Aisha and Nurzhan continued their journey to Lake Balkhash. Legend spoke of a magical fish residing in its depths, believed to grant wishes to those with pure hearts. The friends, standing at the water's edge, cast silent hopes into the clear waters, their dreams intertwined with the shimmering reflections of the Kazakh sun.

Their odyssey led them to the mystical Charyn Canyon, a testament to the enduring nature of Kazakhstan's landscapes. Amidst the towering cliffs, they discovered a cave adorned with ancient drawings depicting tales of resilience and unity. These petroglyphs, etched into the rock by ancestors, spoke of a collective spirit that had withstood the test of time.

As the sun dipped below the horizon over the Caspian Sea, Aisha and Nurzhan realized that Kazakhstan's true magic lay not only in its breathtaking landscapes but in the diversity of its people. The Kazakh culture, a harmonious blend of nomadic traditions and modern influences, stood as a testament to the resilience and adaptability of the nation.

Their journey continued to the cultural crossroads of Shymkent, where Aisha and Nurzhan found themselves amidst the vibrant festivities of a traditional Kazakh wedding. The lively music and swirling dances reflected the celebratory spirit deeply ingrained in Kazakh culture.

They joined the revelry, immersing themselves in the joyous traditions that bridged the gap between the past and the present.

In the historical city of Turkestan, the friends explored the mausoleum of Khoja Ahmed Yasawi, a UNESCO World Heritage site. The intricate architecture, adorned with turquoise tiles, reflected the spiritual legacy of Sufi mysticism. Aisha and Nurzhan, captivated by the tranquil atmosphere, understood that Kazakhstan's cultural mosaic extended beyond the tangible, encompassing spiritual richness and diversity.

As Aisha and Nurzhan embarked on their journey, their bond strengthened with each step they took together. Their friendship, forged in the quiet moments of childhood and tempered by shared dreams, served as the guiding light through the unknown paths ahead. Through laughter and tears, challenges and triumphs, they found solace in each other's company, their unwavering support a testament to the depth of their connection.

The reason behind their journey lay in their shared curiosity and thirst for knowledge. Aisha, with her insatiable appetite for history and culture, yearned to unravel the mysteries of their homeland's past. Nurzhan, with his adventurous spirit and love for exploration, sought to discover the hidden gems scattered across the vast expanse of Kazakhstan. Together, they embarked on a quest to unearth the treasures buried within their heritage and to weave their own stories into the tapestry of their nation's narrative.

Returning to their village, Aisha and Nurzhan became storytellers, sharing the tales of their cultural odyssey with their fellow villagers. They organized gatherings where traditional Kazakh music echoed through the night, fostering a sense of community pride.

As seasons changed and the winds whispered through the steppes, Aisha and Nurzhan realized that their journey was not just a physical exploration but a profound immersion into the soul of Kazakhstan. The intricate blend of nomadic heritage, folklore, and modern influences created a cultural symphony that resonated through the landscapes and the hearts of its people.

And so, in the quietude of the Altai Mountains, Aisha and Nurzhan's story became a chapter in the ever-evolving narrative of Kazakhstan's cultural legacy, a testament to the enduring spirit that binds its people to the vast and timeless landscapes they call home.

We hope that their journey does not end there and they will continue to conquer the sacred steppes and cultures of peoples. I believe that such an adventure will help preserve the memory of our ancestors and the spirit of our steppes.

A Brave Feat

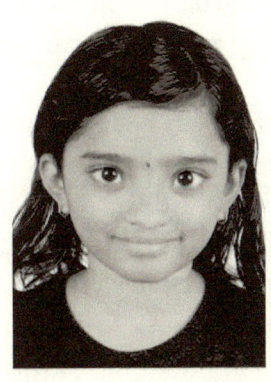

Aditi Oruvannoor
Grade 5
SCS Swaminarayan Academy
Nairobi, Kenya

Bethany had a venturesome soul. She was often daring and didn't like it when she was restrained from doing something. Given her quiet reputation at school, she was very eager to participate in activities. She was a smart girl, and she knew it; in fact she wanted worldwide recognition in it. But there was not so much she could do stuck inside a classroom. The bus was waiting for her to take her home while she was packing her school bag.

When she got back home, she was surprised by the fact that she and her parents were going camping in Naivasha for the weekend! She shuffled through her clothes and hurriedly packed her bag and got into the car. "Why so much of the rush?" she asked still not changed from her school uniform. "Cause if we don't leave right now, we will get there by Monday!", said her mom clearly exaggerating.

Bethany was excited because she had heard many things about Naivasha from her friends. In the heart of Nakuru County, Kenya, lies the town of Naivasha, nestled on the tranquil shores of Lake Naivasha. The town's name is steeped in local tradition, deriving from the Maasai word "ɛnaɨpόsha," meaning "that which heaves." This term vividly describes the lake's surface, which undulates with wave action when the winds blow, or storms gather. Over time, the British settlers, attempting to pronounce this Maasai term, shaped it into the name we know today, Naivasha. Interestingly, this transformation has led to a charming redundancy, as "Lake Naivasha" translates to "Lake Lake," and "Naivasha Town" to "Lake Town."

Naivasha is more than just a name; it's a gateway to adventure and tranquility. The town offers a wildlife sanctuary where visitors can embark on intimate walking tours among zebras, giraffes, and hippos. For those seeking serenity, boat rides on the lake provide opportunities to spot a variety of birds and the occasional crocodile. The nearby smaller, peaceful lake is a haven for birdwatchers and nature enthusiasts, with beautiful birds and hippos all around, painting a perfect picture of harmony and natural beauty.

Going there on the road was long and boring. She slept through most of the ride. Once she reached there her dad started making the tent. It was blue in color and could fit two families. Meanwhile her mom was making a campfire. It was late when everything was set up. They made a quick dinner of noodles and roasted marshmallows.

They all went to bed; it took Bethany some time to sleep after all she slept in the car for most of the journey. She was following her own train of thoughts. Then she noticed the smoke coming inside through the tent's window. After debating with herself whether to go out or stay inside, she finally looked out to see a blazing fire, sparks flying over to nearby trees, and bushes. She ran back into the tent and used her mother's phone to call the fire department. While she was waiting for the fire fighters, she roused her parents from their sleep. They told her to get into the car as it was far from the fire.

The firefighter arrived and put out the fire. Her parents packed the camping gear and joined Bethany in the car. They explained to her that the fire was caught because one log stayed on fire. Her parents also told her that she was getting an award for her bravery and she was being praised around the town. Overwhelmed by this news she thought to herself, it was not worldwide fame but nonetheless it was a good start.

Down from the Mountains

Abraham Meili
Grade 8
Machabeng College
Maseru, Lesotho

They had been here for a year, so everyone knew about them. Everyone wanted to know why they were here. There have hardly ever been any Africans in Gravelbourg, and until then, we had never seen anyone from Lesotho. The villagers had many questions. Most of us had never heard of that country, and we wanted to know more. Questions such as: "Is it hot there?", "What do they eat?" and "Are there many wild animals in that place?" popped into the minds of the inhabitants of this small Saskatchewan town. However, Canadians tend to be too reserved to ask such questions. For the first year, hardly anyone spoke to them. They stayed to themselves, and we stayed to ourselves. All we knew were rumours spread around at Café Paris (that small coffee shop where the women of town spend most of their time).

But the newcomers couldn't stay on their own forever. After all, the family had three children, and everyone knew someone would teach the children. So off to school, they went, a rather good school called "Collège Mathieu." This school has a French name because most of the town consists of French speakers who had established Gravelbourg. They spoke with our children at school, and they reported back to us. The children told us that the strangers came from high up in the mountains of Lesotho, in a tiny village of sheep and goat herders. But our children didn't know then how or why they had come. They could not explain why these people's destinies and dilemmas had forever merged with ours. We did not yet know how big a role these people would play in our lives. We didn't know then that we would suffer together, cry, and laugh with strangers from so far away. We didn't know. All we knew was what the children saw and heard. Perhaps that is always the case.

Only later did we find out why they were here. They had already been here for nearly two years, occupying themselves by learning French and preparing to start working. The children told us that the strangers had studied as doctors in another faraway place: Bloemfontein, South Africa. White doctors in big cities like Moose Jaw and Swift Current sometimes hailed from South Africa; one had even worked in Gravelbourg for a time. He had spoken of Bloemfontein; he claimed to originate from that area. We never understood that doctor, but it is a small place here, and one must take what one gets. Canada often takes foreign doctors and sends them to work in small towns like Assiniboia, Mossbank, and Gravelbourg. We had seen doctors from other African countries but never from Lesotho. Soon, however, Drs Leseli and Mpho started working at Saint Joseph's Hospital in town. They started slowly, just diagnosing a couple of patients with little problems like heartburn or rhinovirus. But gradually, we became increasingly dependent upon them - and grateful. That winter was rough, and our people were taking it hard.

The harvest had been unsuccessful, and people had started to feel it. With six feet of snow on the ground, injuries spread like wildfire, the kind of raging forest fires that burn Northern Saskatchewan in the summer and leave nothing behind. The doctors started working overtime, trying their hardest to keep up with the pace of the town's injuries. Because of this, they were now fully integrated into Gravelbourg life. They chatted at Café Paris after work just like the rest of us and worked themselves to the bone fighting the winter back. But winter brings spring, and March came in like a lamb. We were doing better now, that was good. We thought maybe some of the jobs would come back. We thought it might rain a little more this year, and we would all live for a little longer.

March comes like a lion and goes like a lamb or comes like a lamb and goes like a lion. We thought we had found the exception, but in Saskatchewan, that desolate land of cold that burns and heat that scalds, exceptions do not exist. The winter bit back in the form of disease. Nathaniel Mendoza is a Filipino immigrant in Gravelbourg (many Filipinos work in the trailer factory on the edge of town), and one day, he showed up at Saint Joseph's Hospital with his daughter Rosa in a mess. Mr. Mendoza was well loved in Gravelbourg for his kindness and because he volunteered to help anyone at any time, the hospital was only too ready to accept him. Dr Mpho was on duty, so Rosa and Mr. Mendoza came to her. Mr. Mendoza informed her that Rosa had been having horrid spasms, after which she often fainted. She had a steadily worsening headache and was afraid of light. Dr. Mpho was quick to a diagnosis: "I am sorry, Ntate[1], but it seems that your daughter has tuberculosis meningitis." Nurse Nicole stood there with her mouth ajar. "No!" she said, "never in Saskatchewan! Hasn't it been eradicated?" Having quietly watched this exchange; Mr. Mendoza spoke up. "You know, Ma'am," he said, addressing the nurse, "In the Philippines, we are plagued constantly by this disease." Most cases of tuberculosis in Saskatchewan indeed occur in new arrivals. Still, in countries such as Lesotho and the Philippines, it affects large sectors of the population everywhere. Despite the problems we face here, there are some difficulties we thankfully need not face.

In most cases, tuberculosis meningitis is treatable, but for Rosa, it had gone a long time undiagnosed. We needed to treat her then, or Rosa would die. The doctors and Rosa would have to go to Saskatoon to cure her. Going to Saskatoon was unthinkable for a resident of Gravelbourg. Those who move there never come back to the farms. From there, these former farmers may move on to some even farther and distant cities, such as Toronto or Montreal, and lose themselves there as so many others have before. But that child needed care and fast. So, the doctors decided: "Ntate Mendoza," said Dr. Mpho, "Ntate Leseli and I will take your daughter to Saskatoon, where she will be cared for properly." Mendoza agreed without hesitation. And so off they went. Despite the late hour, the doctors drove to Saskatoon all night. The great city emerged before their eyes as they crossed the bridge and emerged onto the dark grounds of Royal University Hospital. That night, they prayed. To anyone or anything that would listen, they prayed. In Mr. Mendoza's house, they prayed. At church,

1. *Ntate means father or sir in Sesotho, the language of Lesotho, and is used to address adult men. The female equivalent is 'Mme.*

we all prayed, brought together by our love of these people from far away who were now part of our lives. And in the hospital, scared out of her mind in the strange hospital bed, Rosa prayed too. We all prayed that night, praying for the life of one who deserved to live. The next morning, the doctors declared she would live. She would have to spend two weeks in the hospital recuperating, but she would live. She would live to run and cry and laugh with these children from everywhere. She would live under the roof of this nation made of elsewhere, saved by these people who have come down from the mountains to the land of the living skies.

The Noise

Anna Silenchuk
Grade 10
International School of Luxembourg
Luxembourg.

There's always noise. It can be anything really. Birds chirp on sunnier spring mornings, but more often than not, harsh rain drums on the roofs and cars, and blue-grey clouds hang on the horizon. Today is one of those mornings. I pull myself awake and sit on the edge of my bed, trying desperately to rub the sleep out of my eyes, knowing that I need to get up for school. It takes some time. Greyer mornings are harder, but I manage to get out of the house on time.

My walk to school may be short, but every step carries a sense of history and home. Luxembourg is a small but beautiful country in the heart of Europe. It is surrounded by three other countries—Belgium, France, and Germany. People here speak multiple languages, including Luxembourgish, French, and German. The city is filled with modern buildings, but there are also ancient castles and stone bridges that tell stories of the past.

Small, that's what everything is here. The country is tiny, practically the size of a city. It's smaller than Beijing or Istanbul, surrounded by three other countries, with basically no military, but considered a financial hub. If you haven't guessed by now, then maybe you've just never heard of it. Luxembourg has layers to it. The top, the financial sector, and the richest of the rich, who drain life out of this place, are an ever-present force, visible in the clean and modern cities, the big schools whose names are cut out of red and blue plastic and stuck to the sides, and the endless high-end stores. And then there's us. When the layer of suited men, mortgages, and bank statements is peeled back, you see us.

I blast music in my headphones to drown out the construction work and pull my hood over my head to avoid the rain. Once I reach my school, I shake off the water from my clothes, and droplets fly everywhere.

As I walk through our hallway to my friends as usual, I notice something is different. My group is bustling with excitement and worry, with three separate conversations happening at once. There are six of us—Leo, Jesse, Leia, Miles, Emmy, and me. I manage to collect fragments of information from my friends, Jesse and Leia.

There's this place, city, or Luxembourg City, but we just call it city for short. Everything happens there. You can't walk more than a hundred meters without seeing someone you know there. And a lot of people buy and sell things there. Not illegal stuff or anything, just regular products, furniture, electronics, and clothes, just second-hand. It's like a flea market, but unofficial, and everything happens through a "guy." If you want to buy something, you talk to a friend, and he or she finds you a "guy." Then you find time to meet; the "guy" sells you the phone or laptop or whatever you were looking for, and you pay. Pretty simple. Except it's not. With an unofficial system, you get scams. And lots of them.

Our friend Leo is a "guy." He was selling these old basketball jerseys that he and his dad were collecting. His father loved basketball, and these jerseys reminded him of the good times they shared. He was really sad that he had to sell them, but he needed the money, and his dad isn't around anymore, so he picked out a few. Leo had arranged to meet someone in the city to sell the jerseys, but after he left, he never returned. Nobody knew where he was, and now we were all very worried.

"We have to find him," Jesse says, and everyone nods.

We decided to go to the city after school to look for him. When the final bell rang, we rushed out and met up by the bus stop, right next to the kiosk where Miles and Emmy sometimes buy a candy bar to share while waiting for the bus. The buses here are easy; they come every ten minutes, so we're settling into the brownish, crumby seats in no time. And then we're in the city.

As we step off the bus in the city center, the sound of street musicians playing fills the air. We see businessmen walking briskly and tourists admiring the historic monuments. Luxembourg City is a special place, full of both history and modern life. The streets have grand old buildings, but there are also small, cobbled alleyways with colorful graffiti.

We don't know where to begin our search. I look around; there are about three tour groups nearby, so words in foreign languages are floating around us; men in suits walk swiftly, talking on phones; somewhere further on, the sound of a saxophone from one of the many street performers. I turn slowly, looking for nothing in particular, but my gaze focuses on something. A man in cargo shorts and a huge zip-up, with a guitar slung over his shoulder, is sitting on the steps of the stage in the center of the square. It's Ronnie. I don't remember how I even met him, but he knows me, and when he notices me, he waves. I wave back and start walking towards him.

"Maybe he saw Leo!" I say, and we rush over to him.

Ronnie listens carefully as I describe Leo—short, curly black hair, wearing a dark green hoodie. His English is a little dodgy. Through a mix of English, French, and signaling, he tells me we need to go to the bridge on the edge of the city. There's something on his face, though. A look of concern and sadness, and I can tell he is worried.

Jesse lives right in the city, so he takes us down an alley, assuring us it's a shortcut. The rain starts to fall again, big droplets, as we emerge from between the graffiti-covered walls and towards the bridge. There are these monolithic structures, almost like castle ruins, along the sides, and as we cross the bridge, I catch a glimpse of a dark green hoodie.

Leo's sitting down with his legs pressed to his chest. His face looks tired, and there is a small bruise near his eye. His breathing is ragged, like he can't clear his throat. He doesn't look at us. He tries his best not to look at anything. We just stand there on the edge of the road and look at him, and he just sits there. For the first time, there is no noise. Nobody moves; nobody talks; the usual hum of the city disappears. For the first time, everything is silent.

We take the bus back to school and get Leo some water and a candy bar in the convenience store. He doesn't touch the candy bar but drinks all the water as soon as Leia hands it to him. We don't talk; we don't ask what happened, who the man was, or where his jerseys are. Because when something like this happens, you just don't ask. We are just happy he is safe.

After that day, Leo was quieter than before. He didn't smile as much, and he seemed lost in thought often. But we stayed by his side, letting him know that he wasn't alone. Life in Luxembourg continued as usual—buses still arrived every ten minutes, and the city still bustled with life. But for us, something had changed. We had learned that friendship means looking out for each other, no matter what. And sometimes, the best way to help someone is just to be there for them.

Adventures at Raja Tun Uda Library

Tiffany Lee Zi Ching
Grade 9
Nobel International School
Selangor, Malaysia

As the sun rose on the 16th of February, the students at our school, nestled in the heart of Malaysia, buzzing with excitement. It wasn't just another school day; it was a day of exploration, a day to venture beyond the confines of their familiar classrooms and textbooks. For, on this day, they were to visit the illustrious 'Raja Tun Uda Library' in Shah Alam, Selangor.

We were excited because we were going to visit one of the most beautiful libraries in Asia. Raja Tun Uda's library has the concept of "Library in a Garden". The location is very strategic, which is next to the Sultan Abdul Aziz Shah Golf Club. This was the choice of His Majesty Sultan Sharafuddin Idris Shah Alhaj Ibni AlMarhum Sultan Salahuddin Abdul Aziz Shah Alhaj, Sultan of Selangor who wanted the concept of this library in the park.

The timeless adage suggests that to truly gauge a place, go through their library, and you'll learn much about their culture and history, which not only draws from the region's years but also cultivates a culture steeped in literature, community spirit, and the preservation of old-world charm.

Among the eager students was me, along with my fellow library ambassadors. Led by our beloved senior school librarian, Dr. Maya, we embarked on this journey with hearts brimming with anticipation. Unlike the other groups who boarded buses, Dr. Maya's group was lucky enough to travel in a van, and the thrill of the ride heightened our excitement.

As we traversed through the bustling streets, the anticipation bubbled within us. The journey seemed endless, yet each passing minute brought us closer to our destination. Finally, after what felt like an eternity, we arrived at the grand entrance of the Raja Tun Uda Library.

Stepping out of the van, we were greeted by the sight of the magnificent library building, its grandeur captivating our senses. Although exhaustion from the school day weighed heavy on our shoulders, the allure of the library revitalized our spirits.

Led by Ms. Hikmah, one of the knowledgeable librarians at Raja Tun Uda Library, we were briefed on the library's rules and regulations before ascending to the fourth floor for a detailed introduction to the library's history and facilities. It was awe-inspiring to learn that the library had been serving the community for over half a century, offering an array of amenities such as a cafeteria, a theatre, and even a recording room equipped with advanced technology.

The concept of free membership and the opportunity to borrow up to 20 books at a time enthralled us. Moreover, the innovative 'book shower' system, designed to sanitize books, sparked our interest and left us pondering about its potential implementation in our school library.

Though our time was limited, we eagerly explored the vast expanse of the library. We entered rooms filled with historical archives detailing Malaysia's past—ancient manuscripts, old *batik* prints, and even letters from the days of the *Kesultanan Melayu Melaka* (Malacca Sultanate). The meticulous arrangement of these artifacts showcased the nation's dedication to preserving its rich heritage. In the recording room, some of my friends excitedly recorded a podcast discussing their favourite books, using a green screen to enhance their visual effects.

One thing that stood out was the impeccable cleanliness of the library. We admired the attention to hygiene, especially the requirement to remove shoes before entering designated sections - an echo of the *adat melayu* (Malay custom) of keeping spaces clean and respectful.

Guided by our teachers, including Dr. Maya and Ms. Michelle, we navigated through the cataloging room, gaining insights into the meticulous organization of the library's vast collection. Interacting with the friendly staff and learning about their roles filled us with admiration and appreciation for their dedication.

As the day drew to a close and we bid farewell to Perpustakaan Raja Tun Uda, I felt an overwhelming sense of gratitude. This visit had been more than just a school trip -- it was an opportunity to immerse ourselves in a new environment, gain valuable insights, and develop a greater appreciation for the power of knowledge. As I glanced back at the grand edifice, I knew that this wouldn't be my last visit. Someday, I would return to once again lose myself in the magic of books, history, and the beauty of a Library in a Garden.

The True Beauty of Island Life

Zara Ibrahim Rushdhi
Grade 10
GN Atoll Education Centre
Fuvahmulah city, Maldives

In one of the many beautiful and serene islands of the Maldives, lived two sisters, Zainab and Maya. Just a couple of months prior, they used to live in the main city, Male, a concrete jungle where dreams were made. Tall buildings, and the sound of vehicles honking filled the skies of the bustling city which never slept. Realizing that a permanent life in the city might prevent their children from forming a connection with the real culture of Maldives, Zainab and Maya's parents decided to move back to their home island with their children. It was a place where life was slow and the air was filled with the sweet scent of the sea.

Zainab was still getting used to the peacefulness of island life. She didn't fully appreciate the wonders that lay hidden within its shores. Her heart desired to move back to Male, as the city- life was all she had known her whole life. The city was familiar to her, she was used to the liveliness of it. On the other hand, her little sister Maya was quite the opposite. Ever since they moved, Maya has been eager to explore the island. Not a day goes by when Maya does not ask Zainab to take her out to traverse through the sandy pathways of the island.

Zainab did not pay heed to Maya's requests as she felt that the island could not compare to the hustle and excitement of the capital city. But today, Zainab finally agreed to go out with Maya. She didn't know exactly why she said yes. Maybe a part of her did want to uncover the secrets of the island. But she wasn't ready to admit it, at least not yet. Maya's eyes sparkled with excitement as she finally had the opportunity to explore the island and spend time with her sister.

As they ventured out, the warmth of the sun hit Zainab's tan olive skin, and a soft breeze rustled through the palm trees. She felt at ease. It was like the island was whispering in her ears to listen to its beautiful rhythms. Maya skipped ahead of Zainab, her laughter filling the air as she eagerly led the way. Zainab couldn't help but feel a little excited to discover what the island held in store for her.

Their first stop was the beach, where they met a friendly fisherman named Ali. Ali had a warm smile and eyes that twinkled like the stars. He welcomes Zainab and Maya to watch as he casts his net into the salty waters. Maya clapped her hands with joy as Ali pulled up the next, revealing a bright bunch of colorful fish glimmering in the sunlight. Ali shared stories of his adventures at sea, of chasing after schools of fish and navigating through stormy waters with his father ever since he was a little boy. Zainab was captivated by Ali's tales of bravery and resilience.

Next, Zainab and Maya came upon a quaint workshop where a traditional rope maker named Hassan, crafted coir ropes of all shapes and sizes. Hassan's hands worked carefully as he weaved the strands of coir together into strong ropes that could endure the mightiest of storms. Maya and Zainab watched in awe as Hassan worked his magic. He shared stories of the island's history, of fishermen and sailors relying on his ropes for their livelihoods. How his ropes were used by many of the households for various purposes. From hanging clothes to dry out in the sun, to making 'Joali fathi', a traditional roped seat. Zainab listened intently, coming to realize that every knot held a piece of the island's rich history.

As the sun dipped below the horizon of the sea, Zainab and Maya returned home elated after hearing all kinds of different stories. They sat with their mother, recounting the day's adventures over cups of warm black tea. Zainab shared her newfound appreciation for island life, her eyes shining with excitement. In that moment, surrounded by the warmth of her family and the beauty of her home island, Zainab realized that true happiness wasn't found in the hustle and bustle of the city. It was found in the simplest moments shared with loved ones, in the stories told by those who called the island home.

Zainab hugged Maya closely, grateful for the journey that had led them to discover the true beauty of island life. She knew then that she wanted to spend the rest of her life right here, connected to her roots, surrounded by the island's beauty and the love of her family. She was proud to call this island her home.

Whispering Flowers - Where flowers speak the language of heart

Sneha Gurung
Grade 12
Chhorepatan Secondary School
Pokhara, Nepal

It was 8 a.m. when the sunshine passed through the windows of the flower shop in Thapathali, Kathmandu to reach the delicate petals of orchids and allure the fragrant scent of lilies to welcome a beautiful day.

Thapathali is nestled amidst the lush valleys of Nepal. Thapathali means abode of the Thapas. Legend had it that the very roots of this city were intertwined with the illustrious Thapa dynasty.

Mrs. Gurung, the owner of the shop, was opening it up for the day, singing along to her favorite song on the radio. She began by making five distinct bouquets. She stepped back with a satisfied smile to look at her beautiful bouquets, which were ready to convey the unspoken emotions. While anticipating the arrival of her customers, she busied herself with various tasks, yet her gaze inevitably wandered to her exquisite bouquets, patiently awaiting selection.

By the end of the day, they become part of someone's special occasion, a beautiful expression of love, joy, respect, or simply a way to bring a smile to their face. Mrs. Gurung's four bouquets have all found new homes except Dahlias Boutique. She flips the "closed" sign, and she glances towards the dahlia, its orange glow undimmed. A small smile graces her lips. "Maybe tomorrow," she whispers, a silent promise to the waiting flower, and steps out, pulling the door shut with a gentle click. The lingering fragrance of flowers hangs in the air, a sweet reminder of the day's magic.

The chime of the closing door fades into a whispering silence. A soft whispering sound fills the previously thriving shop. It's not the sigh of the air conditioner or the creak of settling floorboards. No, this sound is different. It's the flowers. "Another successful day, spreading sunshine wherever we went." A nearby lily nods its head in agreement. "We may not have the voices that humans understand, but our colors and forms speak volumes." A bloom of wildflowers chimes in, their voices an enchanting melody, and the whispers fill the shop, a symphony of mellow contentment. They share stories of the smiles they sparkled, the tears they pacified, and the celebrations they brightened.

But among the chorus, a single voice is missing. In a quiet corner, a dahlia, full and vibrant with its crown of petals, remains silent. Today, it was not selected unlike its counterparts. A wave of sadness might brush its velvety blooms, longing to be part of the stories whispered around the shop. However, the dahlia is a flower of strength and resilience. It doesn't wilt with disappointment. Instead, it gathers its energy for another day. As the night deepens, the whispers turn into dreams. The roses dreamed of soft touches and whispered promises. The sunflowers visualize themselves relaxing in the morning sun, spreading joy. The dahlia also dreams, albeit with different aspirations. It seeks to be chosen for a purpose that seamlessly aligns with its lively essence.

The chime of the opening door announces the start of a new day. Mrs. Gurung flips the "open" sign with a smile. The morning breeze in Thapathali streets is still heavy with the sweet fragrance of yesterday's blooms, a lingering reminder of the stories whispered in the night. She surveyed the displays; the remaining flowers seemed brighter and more vibrant. Mrs. Gurung approaches the dahlia, her fingers brushing its soft petals. "Perhaps today is your day," she murmured while a knowing smile played on her lips.

The shop door opens, revealing the first customer of the day. The cheery chime seems to echo the hopeful energy that fills the shop. This customer, with a look of concern, approaches Mrs. Gurung. "Good morning," the customer greets with a soft voice. "I'm looking for some flowers to send to a friend who isn't feeling well—something vibrant and hopeful. Maybe something that says, 'Wishing you a speedy recovery'?"

Mrs. Gurung's eyes light up. "We have exactly that kind of flower that you want," she exclaims, turning towards a specific corner of the shop. "Dahlias! They symbolize strength, resilience, and new beginnings—perfect for someone who's sick."

She reaches out and picks up the dahlias. The rich orange color of the dahlias seems to capture the sunlight, filling the shop with a warm glow. The morning sun glints off its vibrant petals, and its healthy form seems to radiate hopeful energy.

"These orange ones are just what I was looking for; they are my friend's favorite flower," the customer says, his voice filled with newfound joy. "They're so vibrant and cheerful, perfect for lifting my friend's spirits." Mrs. Gurung nods in agreement. "Orange dahlias specifically symbolize creativity, happiness, and encouragement. They're a wonderful way to send positive vibes to your friend." She expertly selects a few of the most vibrant orange dahlias, their petals unfurling in all their glory.

As Mrs. Gurung prepares the bouquet, she adds a few sprigs of complementary greenery to balance the look. The customer pays for the beautiful arrangement, a sense of hope replacing his previous worries.

As they exit the shop, the orange dahlias seem to hold a silent promise of brighter days ahead. The dahlia, once kept in a quiet corner, is finally on its way, ready to bring a touch of sunshine and encouragement to someone in need.

Finally, as the day progresses into evening and the shop gets quiet, the last customer exits with a cheerful bouquet. Mrs. Gurung begins to close her shop. Lights are switched off, water is given to thirsty plants, and leftover trimmings are gathered for composting. As she reaches for the "closed" sign, the shop door clicks shut, silencing the daytime symphony. The night settles, and the shop becomes a haven for floral dreams, each flower waiting for its chance to bloom and whisper the language of flowers and hearts.

The story of the dahlia offers a beautiful metaphor for us humans, teaching valuable lessons about perseverance, self-belief, identifying what makes us special, and finding a way to contribute to our beautiful world. Just like the dahlia that finds its perfect match, trust that our time will come. This story can be a reminder that even when things don't go according to plan, patience and resilience can lead to unexpectedly better opportunities.

Silent Whispers of the Hidden Beauty

Agnus Shib
Grade 11
Mount Roskill Grammar School
Auckland, New Zealand

It was a usual evening. While I was preoccupied watching my favorite show 'Friends', my alarm rudely interrupted me, telling me it was 6 o'clock. It struck me that today was the day I had scheduled to climb 'Puketāpapa'. As I was leaving the house, that one picture that drew my eye among all the others that hung on the walls. It was taken when I was 5 years old. My grandmother and I were grinning at the camera with the mountain behind us.

'Puketapapa' is the Māori name for a volcanic cone located in Auckland, New Zealand. In English, it is commonly referred to as 'One Tree Hill'. Puketapapa holds significant cultural and historical importance for the Māori people and is a popular tourist destination in Auckland, offering panoramic views of the city and its surroundings. It is in the suburb that shares its English name, Mount Roskill.

The mountain was formed because of volcanic activity approximately twenty thousand years ago. Its peak, located in present-day Winstone Park towards the southwest end of the suburb, is hundred and ten metres in height. It is one of the many extinct cones that dot the isthmus of Auckland, all part of the Auckland volcanic field. The scoria cone was built by fire-fountaining from two craters. Lava flowed from the base of the cone to the north and to the northwest.

My grandmother adored embarking on adventures. Amongst the many mountains she has climbed is the Puketāpapa. I cherished her stories, which she would often share with me. One day, she told me about her story of climbing Puketapapa.

I began like this,"the sun was slipping off until it was overtaken by the moon, and I discovered the most captivating sight as the moon rose to claim the sky". My mind was tingling with thoughts about what could be that captivating scene.

"Grandma, what was the scene you saw, can you please tell me? " I questioned.

Then she said, " Oh my! what might it be, it was not just any scene; it was a treasure, and you have to find treasure within yourself to recognize what it might be" she said at that moment.

With a blend of curiosity and annoyance, I said, "Nana, remember that one day when I grow up, I'm going to climb Puketāpapa and see the treasure too."

Tears that were running streaming down my face and shifted to follow the sun. I started to walk, estimating that it would take me thirty minutes to reach the mountain. The moment I set foot out into the other setting sun, a startling wind kissed me in the face and sealed me within its embrace only for a moment.

As I walked, the warmth of the sunlight welcomed me as I shuddered against the chilly wind. As I strolled along the road, I saw people giggling, riding and there was a lot of traffic on the motorways due to cars and trucks passing through. I waited for a few minutes after  pressing the pedestrian cross button when I noticed the mountain across the street. Then the light turned green, and I crossed the road to come up in front of an arc. I stared in deep respect and admiration at the elegance of the arc.

Each line that was carved into the arc whispered a different story, making it feel like you were entering a book of fairy tales. The area sky darkened lovely and crowded with people, most of whom were leaving as the moon rose. Walking up, I realized that this was going to be the steepest climb I had ever done. I kept climbing until I eventually reached the top.

As soon as I reached the summit, the sun disappeared, and the show began as the big bright moon opened with twinkling stars all around him, as the streetlights came to life one by one. As they perch quietly watching over the chain of expensive cars and trucks that pass beneath them. Each one stood proudly by removing the lonely darkness with its gentle stream of light. I was stunned as I thought that the stars had ascended on Earth and made the cityscape radiant. These stars have become my secret keepers, who whisper promises of the person I aspire to become. They give me the strength to close my eyes in the darkness and shed tears, safe in the knowledge that their aura will secure my loneliness. I long to ascend the steep hills and reach their scouring sky height, to whisper back that I am there for them as they have been for me, illuminating my path when life's twinkle turned to regrets.

As I looked around me, I couldn't help but admire the enchantment that the streetlights give to the darkness of night. I could tell they were more than just ordinary lamps; they were keepers of the beauty that one can find if they take their time to look into their darkest time. They made the buildings, once impressive and intimidating, bathed in the tender, golden fire. The fire made the world transform into a faded illusion of happiness. The streetlights took me further into the soul of the city. I could feel the way the tears made a road from my eyes to my cheeks and into my dry lips. I tasted the happiness in my tears.

At that moment I knew why my grandmother didn't reveal the treasure to me because if she revealed the treasure, it would never convey its real beauty to me. I said my final goodbye to my stars who made the city a milky way filled with shining and glittering streetlights. The play ended as I closed my eyes against the warmth of my bed, but I could still hear whispers. As they sang to me, it was a song of goodbye to see you again and shower the magnificence of the unknown with a golden fire.

Your Personal Choice

Oluwabukayo Micheal Adeyeye
Grade 11
Rhemal Chapel International
Ibadan, Nigeria

I lay awake all night remembering those sweet lullabies mum used to sing to me at bedtime. I can't recall the lyrics, but the melodies still ring eternal bells in my mind's ears. Oh, those glorious, sweet moments. I grew up to tag it "Moments with Mum."

Sometimes, dad would walk into my room with his baritone voice, teasing me till I slept off in his arms. Those are days I always pray not to forget even in old age. I didn't have to bother myself with anything concerning decision-making or making choices. I had them all figured out for me. My parents were simply the best anyone could have.

My first day in school was just a tough one. It was the first time I would stay away from my parents for several hours. Of course, my nanny wouldn't come close to me when my parents were around because auntie Felicia, as I used to call my nanny, knew so well that my attachment to my parents was something she couldn't do anything about.

No matter how hard she tried to please me, it never worked. It was either my parents or no one else. I am sure you know this feeling that comes with being the only child of wealthy parents, the almighty Chief Douglas and Yeye Steicy Afolabi, the influential revered by high-ranking politicians and traditional rulers.

My parents weren't directly in power, but they controlled power at the top. That feeling gave me so much confidence, that attitude of "nothing would happen." I didn't even care to know if other kids' parents were wealthier. Never!

My mum was Igbo while my dad was Yoruba. As I got older, my parents gradually introduced me to cultural tolerance by talking me into spending time in my maternal home. I didn't understand any bit of Igbo language. I didn't even deem it fit to learn any bit of it from Chinedu, my friend in school who was fond of speaking vernacular with his parents whenever they came to pick him up from school.

But for the fact that my school was this reserved environment for exceptional kids, I would have thought that Chinedu was an "olodo." That was the first Yoruba word I learnt. But guess what? When I eventually found out that the meaning of "olodo" was insulting, I felt like apologizing to all those I ever used that word on. I learnt how to stop the use of that word the hard way. My nanny was to help me with my homework on Quantitative and Verbal Reasoning. I discovered that she couldn't attempt any of the questions. It was really a difficult one. So, as she spent the whole time trying to rack her brain for answers, I sighed deeply and called her "olodo." In a swift reaction, she raised her hand to spank me, but she couldn't and so she held her hand in the air for some minutes. Unknown to me, my mum, who was just walking into the house overheard me call my nanny "olodo."

Mum was so nice with her punishment, but I learnt serious lessons from it. She calmly asked me about the meaning of "olodo" and who taught me the word. I told her I learnt it from my peers in school. Most of them used the word to describe other students who couldn't do something well.

"Bella," mum calmly called me. "You see that word you just used on your nanny you will go on your knees and apologise to her now." "Mum! Are you serious?" I asked in sheer disbelief.

She didn't raise her voice at me, she calmly ordered "now!" Staring at her face in shock, I went on my knees and tendered an unreserved apology to my nanny. My mum made it a point of duty to stand by and watch me do it. Thereafter, she told me that for a week I will be taking food and drinking water to my nanny in her room. "It is your turn to serve," she ordered.

I carried out her assignment for the first three days and I must confess that it was not funny. Then I understood the challenging nature of my nanny's work. Auntie Felicia was not just serving me food and drinks, she was doing the same for the whole family and that included when there were visitors. She was the last to go to bed every day. She was even helping me to serve my punishment.

Of course, my mum reported me to my dad who immediately endorsed the punishment she had already given me. So, from that day, I stopped using that word or any other insulting word on anyone. At school whenever my peers used such saucy words, I would educate them on the meaning of the word and how bad it was to use such words. I grew fond of my nanny after that incident.

During Christmas vacation that year, my parents announced my first trip to the East to visit my maternal home. I was frozen to my bones because I had no idea how I was going to cope. I kept staring at Auntie Felicia hoping she was going to appeal against my parents' decision on my behalf, but she only smiled and turned her face away. Later that evening, I went to her in her room asking her to draw up a list of the things I could face during the holiday. She laughed so hard that my parents could hear her laughter from the living room. In any case, she tutored me on how to go to the stream to fetch water, use firewood to cook, and all that.

"Me, cook?" I yelled.

"Yes, you, cook!" Auntie Felicia retorted.

I braced up for the challenge and got set for the journey. I had thought that my parents would drop me off or at least book a flight for me. But no! I was literally billed to the East. My grandma whom I was meeting for the second time was already at the bus terminal to pick me up. It was exhausting but I enjoyed the journey anyway.

I settled in quickly and grandma began her lectures on the decent behaviour expected of the girl-child. She taught me culturally acceptable norms for girls. I was just in another Social Studies/Sociology class. Unknown to me, my parents kept a daily check on me, wanting to know how I was doing. The only day dad spoke with me on the phone during the holidays was when he asked me for an essay to be written on my holiday in the East.

Simply put, all around me, I had strict disciplinarians who wouldn't condone nonsense. I grew up to realise that I was raised well. But somehow, I wanted to experience my own freedom. I wanted to make decisions for myself. The fangs of adolescence fingered my mind. Peer pressure came mounting. Then Ola introduced the idea of having a boyfriend.

I had no idea that Ola introduced her boyfriend to me. The game plan was to use me to steal money from my parents. So, they introduced the idea of self-kidnap. So, I played along. I had abandoned my sincere friends who started avoiding me because of the new company I kept. But there was this thought that kept ringing in my head. The idiomatic expression used by our Literature teacher. He often said that "The child is father of the man." The meaning of this is that whatever character anyone puts up will follow the person all through life.

I ignored that prompting and joined the gangs. Occasionally, my parents' love and care would cross my mind, my nanny's endless love would filter through, but I blocked all that from my mind.

The call was finally put through to my parents about my kidnap. In flip seconds security personnel were deployed everywhere in search of me. The ransom demand was fifty million naira and we were going to share the money equally. In less than 6 hours, my dad called the line of the "kidnappers" announcing that the money was ready. We jumped up in jubilation for the success of evil, well done. Thirty minutes later, we were rounded up by police officers who had been listening to our conversations. We were arrested. My parents were worse than disappointed. I was searching my mind for cogent excuses, but none came. The only thought that settled in was you are a product of YOUR OWN CHOICE!

Echoes of Salalah

Aarif Muhammed Rawther
Grade 10
Indian School Salalah,
Oman

As the sun dipped behind the crimson hues of the Arabian Sea, a gentle breeze whispered through the streets of Salalah, carrying with it the essence of twilight. In accordance with the Omani Government's decree, the buildings of Oman stood adorned in hues reminiscent of the land's rich history, blending harmoniously with the natural palette of Salalah, where shades of white and light brown echoed the mountains and sea.

At the ancient shores of Haffa beach, memories danced in the minds of Fathima and Safwan, transporting them back twenty-five years to their days at the Indian School Salalah. Despite coming from diverse backgrounds, they forged a deep friendship, bonded by shared riddles, academic pursuits, and playful competitions.

When the school announced a picnic to explore Salalah's treasures, excitement surged among the students. Fathima and Safwan reveled in the beauty of Mughal beach, Darbat's lush greenery, and the majestic Zeek mountains, whose misty peaks resembled verdant tea estates. They marveled at the Samharam Mountains, the Sinkhole of Tawi Attair, and the ancient sites steeped in the history of trade between India and Oman.

Amidst laughter and dreams, Fathima expressed her desire to explore the world by sea, prompting Safwan to playfully declare himself her future captain. Little did they know that fate would soon chart their paths apart. Safwan pursued his studies abroad on a scholarship, while Fathima remained in Salalah, embracing her role as a teacher.

Years later, a chance reunion at an Iftar gathering brought Safwan and Fathima back together. With a heartfelt invitation, Safwan arranged to meet Fathima at Haffa beach, where he knelt before her, offering a ship model and a question that would change their lives forever.

In a moment that seemed ordained by the divine, Fathima's tear-filled eyes reflected the culmination of a lifelong bond. United by destiny's hand, they embarked on a journey of love and companionship, choosing to remain unmarried in accordance with their belief in God's will.

Settling in Salalah, Safwan found solace in the warm embrace of its people and the tranquil beauty of its landscapes. Together, in a home painted in the colors of their shared dreams, they nurtured a relationship built on love, trust, and mutual respect, their hands intertwined like the timeless melody of waves upon the shore.

Unity in Diversity

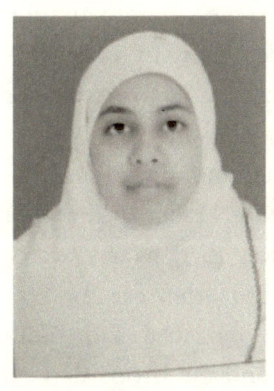

Umaima Yousaf
Grade 9
Siddique Public School
Islamabad, Pakistan

There is a small village nestled between the rolling hills of rural Pakistan. Its name is Gulshan. There lived three best friends: Ali, Maria, and Raj. They are inseparable despite coming from diverse backgrounds – Ali belongs to a Muslim family, Maria to a Christian family, and Raj to a Hindu family.

Gulshan is primarily a residential area with a mix of commercial zones. The village is famous for the natural beauty of rural or mountainous areas of Pakistan. Gulshan is well-known for its vibrant community and urban environment. There are several characteristics of Gulshan that contribute to its charm and uniqueness.

Gulshan is a harmonious place where the call to prayer echoes alongside the church bells and the soft hum of mantras from the nearby temple. In this village, people from various backgrounds live together in peace, sharing their joys and sorrows.

Now, let us return to the lives of our three friends Ali, Maria, and Raj. Ali was a quick-witted boy with a mischievous smile, Maria was known for her kindness and infectious laughter, while Raj had a passion for storytelling and adventure. They spent their days exploring the fields, climbing trees, and chasing butterflies. Each evening, they gathered near the ancient banyan tree, their secret meeting spot, to share stories and dreams.

One scorching summer day, trouble knocked on the door of Gulshan. A severe drought struck the village, drying up the once-gushing river and withering the crops. The villagers grew anxious as their livelihoods were threatened. Fear and uncertainty crept into the usually peaceful community.

Ali, Maria, and Raj could not bear to see their families worried. Determined to help, they decided to seek advice from the village elder, Baba Akbar, a wise man known for his counsel.

Baba Akbar welcomed the trio warmly and listened intently to their concerns. "Children," he said with a serene smile, "unity in diversity is our strength. Each of you brings unique perspectives. To solve this, we must come together, just like the colours of a rainbow."

Inspired by Baba Akbar's words, Ali, Maria, and Raj rallied the village. They organized a communal effort, where Muslim, Christian, and Hindu families joined hands to dig trenches to conserve water, shared whatever little food they had, and prayed together for rain.

Days turned into weeks, and just when hope began to fade, dark clouds gathered in the sky. Thunder rumbled, and raindrops danced on the parched earth. The villagers cheered as the heavens opened, blessing the land with a downpour.

The once-dry river began to flow again, and the fields gradually revived. Gulshan blossomed once more, and the unity shown during hardship only strengthened the bonds between its diverse residents.

As the village rejoiced in the rain's blessings, Ali, Maria, and Raj sat under the banyan tree, gazing at the vibrant rainbow stretching across the sky. They knew that despite their differences, their friendship had not only saved their village but had also painted a beautiful story of unity and togetherness.

And so, in the heart of rural Pakistan, the tale of three friends from different faiths who united their village in a time of need became a legend, reminding everyone that compassion, understanding, and unity can overcome any challenge life presents.

A Tale of Survival and Hope

Sara Mohammed Shubair
Grade 6
Al Remal Middle School for Girls
Gaza, Palestine

In the heart of conflict, amidst the cacophony of chaos and the tremors of uncertainty, Sara's life unfurled like a fragile tapestry, woven with threads of resilience and moments of fleeting tranquility.

Before the tumult of October 7th shattered their world, Sara's days danced to the rhythm of familiarity. Each morning, she ventured to school, her steps buoyed by youthful optimism. The return home marked a sacred ritual of familial unity, where laughter mingled with the aroma of home-cooked meals, and dreams intertwined with the bonds of love. The sea beckoned as a sanctuary, offering solace in its azure embrace, while the streets echoed with the laughter of children and the melody of shared joy.

But destiny, with its capricious whims, tore apart the fabric of normalcy, plunging Sara and her kin into the abyss of war. Rocket sounds shattered the dawn, scattering their hopes like fragile petals in the wind. With each explosion, fear casts its long shadow, etching lines of worry upon youthful faces.

In the crucible of conflict, Sara discovered reserves of strength she never knew existed. Days blurred into nights, punctuated by the symphony of bombs and the relentless rhythm of survival. Yet, amidst the chaos, bonds of kinship grew stronger, their collective resolve a beacon of defiance against the darkness that threatened to consume them.

Forced to flee, they embarked on a journey fraught with peril, seeking refuge in unfamiliar lands. In Khan Yunis, amidst the ebb and flow of uncertainty, they forged a new home from the ashes of their past. The taste of roasted corn mingled with the bitter tang of loss, as they mourned the absence of loved ones who fell prey to the merciless tide of war.

But even in the darkest of nights, hope glimmered like a lone star amidst the tempest. In Rafah, they found sanctuary beneath the canvas of makeshift shelters, where stories were shared like precious treasures, and laughter echoed like a balm for wounded souls.

As the wheels of time turned, they bid farewell to the ravaged shores of Gaza, embarking on a journey towards distant horizons. In Egypt, they found respite from the storm, and in the embrace of the United Arab Emirates, they found a new beginning.

Yet, amidst the opulence of their newfound home, Sara carried with her the echoes of resilience that defined her journey. For in the crucible of conflict, she learned that amidst chaos, there exists a quiet strength that binds us all together—a strength born not of steel and stone, but of the indomitable spirit that resides within the human heart.

In the serene embrace of the United Arab Emirates, Sara found solace in the simple pleasures long denied to her—a taste of ice cream on a sweltering day, the laughter of children echoing through verdant parks, and the warmth of familial love that transcended the trials of the past.

Yet, amidst the comfort of her new surroundings, Sara never forgot the lessons learned amidst the ruins of war. Each day was a testament to the resilience of the human spirit, a reminder that even in the darkest of times, hope could be found in the unlikeliest of places. And as she looked towards the future, Sara carried with her the echoes of her past—a testament to the strength of the human heart in the face of adversity.

The Orient Pearl

Riona Krizzia Abon
Grade 5
St. John the Baptist Catholic School
Malolos, Philippines

Abigail, a high school graduate, was searching through her old belongings.

She saw what she never expected to see—a pearl necklace! Her eyes widened in shock! "Hmm, who would put such a costly thing here?" After minutes straight of thinking about who it could be, a person came into her mind—her great-aunt Livia! "Wait, could it be?" Her great-aunt, Livia, lives on the island of Palawan. "Yes, it must be great, Aunt Lucia! Her place is very well-known for South Sea pearls!" "But wait, she was known for being a medium physicist!" She quickly ran to grab her phone and call her mother. "Mom, I found something unexpected." "What is it?" The curious mother asked. "A pearl necklace!" "How and where did you find it?" Abigail replied, "I was searching across my old stuff, and then I found this, you know, the old brown box with the name 'Abbie'? And oh, whose is it from?" A quick shift appalled the mother's tone. "I didn't know you would find this out this quick." "What?" She was confused. "I'll see you soon, Abigail." Before she could even say something, the call ended.

Days passed by, and as she was sitting on her Narra chair, she could not help but think about the necklace. She thought to herself, "Great Aunt Livia was known for being a medium and even magic! If that necklace were here, could it be that there's magic in it? If so, what kind, though? Plus, she passed away many years ago, so probably it was here the whole time."

One fortunate night, as she was doing her project, she heard a tiny voice! "Mayan, Mayan, Mayan," she stumbled with great fear. "Who? Who are you? Show yourself-!" She looked around and found nothing!

That is when she noticed the necklace, shining through the night on

its pearly whites. An eerie voice echoes across the dark room, with a lampshade being the only source of stable light.

"Mayan, Mayan." She could not understand what it was saying. Is it calling out to somebody? It once again spoke, calling out her name, "Abigail." Her eyes widened with fear! "What? What are you?" "The truth." Again, she could not understand. What truth? She nervously picked up the pearl necklace and asked, "What are you talking about?" "Have you not known yet? You are Mayan." Abigail was frightened. "Who?!" She nervously chuckled. "Eh, well, pearls aren't trustworthy, aren't they?" She dropped it and slowly started backing off. Then, "AHH-!" The pearl had mysteriously moved behind her! "What are you? You are scaring me." "I am Perla, and I'm the key to finding yourself." "Finding? Myself?" Abigail thought about it for a while. "N-no, I'm not easily giving in!" Something shook her; she felt dizzy, and everything was pitch black for a moment. Hmm, was it all a dream? She woke up, gasping for air. "No! This could not be real!" She looked at the necklace. "Maybe I should go visit the church." She told herself, and there she went to Barasoain Church.

After the mass, she met an old lady. "Excuse me... Mayan...", she spoke. Abigail looked at the old lady, and she recalled the pearl necklace that called her the same. She tried to speak with a smile: "Yeah, miss, it is me, Mayan." The old lady's face lit up with joy. "Oh Mayan! I have been looking for you for a long time! Come, others are waiting." She followed the lady into an old Nipa hut in a forest not known to her. She met a group of other young ladies: Josefina, Georgia, and Mayumi. "I have brought before you, our Mayan." The ladies gazed at her, but one seemed off-Mayumi. Abigail eventually became drawn to the pristine environment, as if someone had put a spell on her.

Time flew swiftly, and Abigail, who is now known as "Mayan," On one day, on the feast of Flores de Mayo, one lady instructed Mayan to bring the "Hamayan" necklace. She could not understand it at first until she realized it was the pearl necklace that she had found in her belongings. On her way home to bring the necklace, to her surprise, a lot of missing posters with her name and photographs were posted along. "What has happened...?" She thought. Abigail passed through the streets and heard a familiar voice calling out a name: "Abigail! Has anyone seen Abigail Martinez?" and another one, "She has been missing for 7 months; if you have seen her, please contact us!"

Hearing this, her mind was full with mixed emotions. As she was about to call out, a hand grabbed her from behind. "Abigail!", She looked carefully at the woman's face. " Mayumi! What are you doing here?" Mayumi looked around and said, "You are not Mayan." Abigail's eyes widened. "I'm not...?" She muttered. "You aren't. And you are not meant to be. The real Mayan has been long banished, according to the legend." "According to the legends...?" "Mayan is a Catalonian from the earliest of times; she was said to be powerful, and many others have wanted to claim her power. In a thirst for power, they banished her. Yet some still believe that Mayan still lives in the body of a young woman, and they thought it was you."

"They thought it was me?" She muttered once again.

"Take the necklace you said you had found; take it to the nearest forest, where our Nipa Hut is. Hit it with a stone and burn the remains."

Abigail did as Mayumi said, after crushing it, a white light from above rayed over her face. She saw her whole life before her, like a rewind in a show. Everything blacked out. When she woke up, she was in bed, overlooking the beautiful beach of Siargao from the glass window where she lives. She rushed up to check on everything! It was the same date and time when she was supposed to search through her old belongings.

The Tides of Trouble

Niranjan A K
Grade 9
Ideal Indian School
Doha, Qatar

This is the final call for Ram Shankar, traveling to Hamad International Airport, Doha." The announcement echoed throughout the airport for what felt like the fifth time. Just when the irritated airport staff prepared to announce it again, an unexpected response came.

With a loud bang, the restroom door swung open. Passengers turned their heads in curiosity as a man in his 30s walked out seemingly out of nowhere. Dressed in a three-piece suit with a black coat and a white vest, he had patches of white hair peeking through his artificially dyed dark locks. His long hair occasionally fell across his spectacles, impairing his view. To add to the amusement, one side of his glasses was broken, making them appear as if they were held together by nothing.

"Wait! I'm here!" he shouted, striding confidently past a sea of astonished stares. Approaching the airport staff, he announced, "I think the Ram Shankar you keep calling is me."

"I had a slight issue, you see; the doorknob was stuck, but it's all sorted now." With that, he pulled something resembling a ball from his pocket and placed it on the counter — a broken doorknob.

This quirky introduction gave the other passengers a vivid hint of the escapades they might soon learn about. But for now, let's rewind and explore how this gentleman arrived in such an amusing predicament.

Ram Shankar was a senior executive for a multinational corporation that produced air conditioning units. Following rapid company growth, they sent representatives abroad to analyze sales records. It was clear that sending someone like Ram was a less-than-stellar idea.

On the flight, he managed to achieve a series of blunders: spilling two glasses of apple juice on his co-passenger, bursting a child's balloon — leading to a chorus of sobs from upset kids — pushing someone while tripping in the aisle, and, to top it all off, breaking the lavatory's doorknob.

The First Tide: Upon arriving in Qatar, Ram found himself immersed in a mix of cultures. The airport bustled with travelers from around the globe: British, Indians, Pakistanis, Algerians, Filipinos, and many more. In the crowd, he spotted a man clad in a white robe and black sunglasses, proudly holding the company banner. Ram approached him and introduced himself.

"I believe you're looking for me." "Ram Shankar," the man pronounced with noticeable difficulty. "Yeah, that's right." "Ohh… Assalamualaikum! How are you?" the man greeted him with a deep voice. Not comprehending, Ram looked puzzled. The man, whose name was Ahmed, explained, "Sorry, brother. Assalamualaikum is our greeting, much like 'hello' in your culture."

Ahmed was eloquent and engaging, quickly telling Ram about his life. Originally from Egypt, he had been in Qatar for twenty years, married with four kids, and working as the branch manager.

After a short while, they arrived at the baggage claim. The carousel was crowded with impatient travelers, and Ahmed stepped away to take a call. Just as he returned, a comical scene unfolded before them.

A traveler had inadvertently grabbed the wrong bag and was now sprinting alongside the conveyor belt, resembling someone on a wild ride. After several laps around the carousel, Ram managed to yank out his bag, which sent him barreling into a crowd of unsuspecting passengers and stirred up a flurry of errant luggage. Apologies flowed from Ahmed as they navigated through the chaos.

The Second Tide: Stepping out into the Middle Eastern heat felt like being wrapped in a warm blanket. The blinding sunlight made it hard to see, and Ram quickly began to sweat. Observing his discomfort, Ahmed chuckled. "Brother, the Middle East isn't that hot."

Confused, Ram didn't grasp the meaning until they reached their transport. He soon realized that everything in Qatar was air-conditioned — schools, buildings, and cars all enjoyed this luxury. This explained why their company thrived in such a climate.

As they drove through the city, adorned with vibrant flowers and towering buildings, Ahmed beamed with pride. Qatar appeared to be on par with developed nations, and during the late morning, the streets seemed to hold no one.

A little while later, Ram found himself lounging in a stunning villa, but trouble sparked once again. Mistaking the automatic shower for a manual device, he applied too much force to the control. Water shot out at a high velocity, drenching walls, furniture, and paintings. The villa turned into an indoor waterfall. It was yet another incident requiring a slew of apologies and a replacement for the water-logged decor.

The Third Tide or Tsunami: For the first time, Ram felt guilty that someone had to keep apologizing for his clumsiness, prompting him to tread carefully the following days. The sales report was well received, and meetings went off without a hitch — a brief respite before what was to come.

During a meeting, the CEO of the Middle East division praised Ram and invited him to a party. However, the glamorous gathering he imagined turned out to be quite different.

The venue was a vast tent in the desert, near a tranquil lake… a far cry from the formal setting he had anticipated. Ahmed noticed Ram's confusion. "You were expecting something else, weren't you? This is how we celebrate."

"This is called a Majlis." Descending to the ground, Ram took a seat on a cushion. The CEO approached him with a cup of dark coffee. "This is Kava. We typically enjoy it with dates," Ahmed explained as they settled in.

Ahmed then offered, "Later this evening, we'll have a campfire. The CEO is incredibly wealthy and owns a sprawling farm," pointing towards an expanse that likely housed over 150 camels. "Why not go check out how they set up the campfire? It's quite a sight!"

As the night unfolded, everyone enjoying themselves, the ground suddenly shook. Rushing outside, they were met with complete chaos. Apparently, a man in a suit had attempted to teach camels how to start a campfire.

Clearly, this was a job only someone with immense foresight could handle. The camels broke through their confines, embarking on a frenzied escape through the desert, sending dust flying everywhere. Ahmed watched as the CEO, now overwhelmed, joined in the ridiculous chase.

After witnessing half of his wealth scatter, no one would have blamed the CEO for losing his composure, all thanks to a man whose affinity for three-piece suits and doorknobs seemed to know no bounds.

Magic Plow

Elizaveta Denisova
Grade 6
State Educational Institution School
Moscow, Russia.

Before reading that book, I knew little about folktales and old Russian life. I didn't realize how valuable such tales were until my friend recommended it.

Near the Moskva River in western Russia lies Moscow, the nation's cosmopolitan capital. My school is in the bustling heart of Moscow, near the majestic Red Square. The Kremlin, the historic core of the city, houses tsarist treasures, while the surrounding Red Square symbolizes Russia's rich history.

Yet, today's Moscow is not just a political or cultural hub—it's a modern metropolis. But far beyond its grandeur lies a different world,

captured in folktales—one that tells of wisdom, hard work, and values passed down through generations.

The Tale of the Hardworking Peasant

Long ago, beyond the towering Altai mountains and endless fields, there lived a kind and hardworking peasant. He wasn't a tsar or a noble, just a simple man who worked the land. He lived in a picturesque house on a hill, near a vast forest. The house had stone walls, carved gates, and shutters painted with suns, moons, and stars.

Around the house bloomed a rose garden filled with rare varieties, including mysterious black roses. On the other side stood an orchard, bursting with life. The peasant tended his garden with love, and it rewarded him with lush blossoms in spring and a bounty of apples in autumn.

As the years passed, the peasant's efforts bore fruit. One day, he called his three sons to distribute his inheritance.

To the eldest, he gave the house and the rose garden, instructing him to care for it with his future wife. To the middle son, he bequeathed the orchard, urging him to nurture the trees. To the youngest, he gave a humble mill, an old horse, and a plow. Before parting, the peasant imparted his wisdom:

"To achieve greatness, you must work diligently, protect what you have, and strive to leave a legacy."

A year passed, and the results of their efforts became evident. The eldest son neglected the house; its beauty faded into disrepair. The middle son abandoned the orchard, dismissing the effort required to grow and sell apples.

But the youngest son cherished his plow and his father's advice. With dedication, he tilled the land and grew crops. Over time, he built a bakery, crafting bread so delicious that people traveled from far and wide to buy it. His fame spread, and his brothers, consumed by envy, demanded to know his secret. The youngest told them his plow was magical. Believing this, they stole it one night, hoping to share in his prosperity.

The brothers soon discovered that the plow alone brought them no fortune. Meanwhile, the youngest bought a new plow and continued working tirelessly. When the brothers realized their mistake, they came to him, repentant.

He forgave them and shared the true secret of his success:

"It's not the plow that is magical, but the work you put into it. To reap the rewards, you must sow, nurture, harvest, and create with care."

The brothers took his lesson to heart. They revived the orchard and the rose garden, learning to value hard work. Together, the three sons flourished, and their father's legacy lived on.

Folktales may seem fantastical, but they carry timeless lessons. Now, I cherish them and recommend them to my friends, for they teach us that greatness lies not in magic, but in effort and perseverance.

Safe Place

Fathima Zehra Samir
Grade 12
International School Riyadh
Saudi Arabia

She was lost in the darkness, trying to find a ray of light to save herself from the cruel grasp of the darkness that consumed her. She fell hard, tripping over her favorite toy, and wept silently, unable to see where she was bleeding from. She had been told, "Kiddo, you shouldn't make noise because you never know who might be listening to your hidden screams of agony and take you away from us to a worse place than this darkness."

She believed that darkness was normal and that she was exaggerating, making a fool out of herself. As she crawled further, she felt a bandage lying around. She picked it up and looked around, hoping for someone to come and help her. But she waited for so long, fearing that if she bandaged herself, no one would notice a bleeding child in the darkness.

Still, she waited for a long time until the blood clotted and started to heal, exposed to the cruel world that she knew. She picked up her toy and continued walking.

She saw a swing in the dim light and was excited to finally see the world her teddies used to talk about when she tried to sleep under her blanket to create more darkness. Her favorite toys, Momo and Dodo, two teddy bears who constantly withered, bickered, laughed, loved, their conversations served as her bedtime stories and lullabies. But one day suddenly, Momo and Dodo started arguing, Momo was so scared she pressed herself deep into her pillow to muffle their voices. Many years ago, when she was a child, she thought she was dying after tripping on a metallic chain and cutting herself deeply. She thought the pain might go away after she was done crying or staying silent for some time, but it didn't, it just became worse. As a little kid she completely freaked out, she thought she was going to die without knowing how a rainbow looked like. Her whole world fell apart that day. Her wound turned out fine by just leaving a tiny scar behind and she did not die. As a child, she loved the stars, and her yearning for light was natural, just as her attraction to distant, inaccessible light was typical of a passive dreamer. She just wanted someone to reassure her and tell her that everything would be fine. She dreamed of lying by a slow river, gazing at the light in the trees, free from bickering voices, learning by being nothing, and yet she felt as if she died a few times before truly living.

As the little girl grew up, she left the darkness behind, she knew how colorful the rainbow was, and found happiness in the little things around her. She would lay on a trampoline at night, gazing at the stars, imagining a swing descending from the heavens that would carry her to space, where gravity wouldn't affect her anymore. In a way, she missed the darkness that had sheltered her, even though it had left her to face the harsh realities of life. She had grown accustomed to finding comfort in the silence and pain of the darkness. She was always eager to know how life would be without the familiar darkness, but once she was out of her safe bubble, she felt raw and exposed as if someone stripped her into several pieces which caused the painful realization of how bitter reality is.

Her life was completely evolving, but the only thing that remained the same was, she still slept to the faded voice of her favorite teddies.

Once upon a time, not long ago, she pleaded with someone she loved to love and care for her the way she loved them. One fine day she asked Momo while her eyes ached due to the unshed tear, "You are my home, at least you are supposed to be my home, don't you understand that Momo ?" Momo in return whispered something she couldn't catch, as if the air carried away both the murmured and unspoken words to protect her heart from shattering.

She eventually had to part ways with Momo and return to the darkness, becoming the little, fragile girl she once was. She held in so much for so long that she eventually exploded, suffering silently while appearing perfect to others. She wished more people would check in on her, just as she did for them, but she realized she had to take charge of her own life.

She learnt the fact that only a few people heard her when she was the quietest and that she wouldn't remain sad forever. One day, she would find the light again, unafraid of tripping, because she now knew how to heal herself.

***

As Charles Dickens once said, "A thing constructed can only be loved after it is constructed, but a thing created is loved before it exists."

From Prince to Saint

Iva Brajević
Grade 10
Stefan Dečanski' Primary School,
Belgrade, Serbia

An evening of a January day at Belgrade. I'm leaving the classroom trying to get numbers and the sound of the school bell out of my head. I'm looking forward to the feeling of fresh winter air and wind in my hair.

In the heart of southeastern Europe lies the bustling capital of Serbia, Belgrade. It's a city with a history as rich and varied as the currents that meet at its shores. Standing proudly at the juncture of the Danube and Sava rivers is the Beogradska Tvrđava, a formidable fortress that has witnessed the ebb and flow of empires across the ages.

As the sun sets, casting a golden hue upon its ancient walls, one can't help but feel the weight of history that permeates every stone. Once a pivotal stronghold for the Roman, Byzantine, Ottoman, Serbian, and Austrian empires, the fortress stands as a silent sentinel, bearing witness to centuries of conquest and conflict.

But amidst the echoes of the past, there's a vibrant energy that pulses through the city. Within the walls of the fortress, now home to several museums, lies Kalemegdan, a sprawling park where locals and tourists alike gather to bask in the beauty of the present moment.

It's here, amidst the blend of old and new, that the true essence of Belgrade reveals itself. A city steeped in history yet pulsating with life—a testament to the resilience of its people and the enduring spirit of a place where East meets West at the crossroads of time.

My thoughts get interrupted by a sound. Familiar notes are reaching me – "Uskliknimo s ljubavlju" (Cheer up with love). Yes, It's the anthem about Saint Sava. Children are singing, their voices are echoing around the halls. My thoughts get interrupted by a sound.

Familiar notes are reaching me – "Uskliknimo s ljubavlju" (Cheer up with love). Yes, It's the anthem about Saint Sava. Children are singing, their voices are echoing around the halls.

I am pausing by a panel, looking at portraits drawn by students from our school. I'm pausing and without saying a word I'm telling him that I am the one of many children who gladly learn and sing songs about him or write essays. I'm telling him that every 27th January his name and work are mentioned in my school with great respect. Many thoughts and feelings are getting mixed in my head while I'm looking at his portrait, it seems like he's smiling at me and that his halo's shining brighter than before. I know, it brightens up a path for me and everyone in our school.

I feel pride and happiness. I could write much more, telling

you about the character and deeds of Saint Sava. Everything I have learned and read is facts that we all know. We know that he was the first Serbian archbishop, that he built churches and monasteries, schools and hospitals. But my feeling, while standing in front of his picture, is leading me to analyze his character from another angle.

I clearly see Sava's parents, Stefan Nemanja and princess Ana. I feel their joy when they got their sons, their heirs. I see parents who wish to raise, educate, give them the country to rule. They probably didn't think that the youngest Rastko didn't like those plans. I see his mother's tears, his father's prayers to come back home...But nothing stopped him. He rejected wealth and went down the path of spirituality. I can't stop thinking about his strength. Was he hesitant? Why did he, as the son of wealthy parents, leave the throne when he could live the life of a wealthy spoiled prince? Why did he follow that path? I am going to find answers to my questions in the books. They are saying: His faith in God decided his path, his willpower and persistence". But I would say that young Rastko was chosen, chosen by God.

And today, in my school it's joyful and festive. In every corner there is a holiday feeling. We, proud students, descendants of Saint Sava get on stage, singing and reading, believing that every said verse will come to Saint. That's why we pray to him today, to help us grow in respectful and honest people, just like he was. We pray to him to give us wisdom. To show us the right path, path of knowledge, truth, faith and harmony.

Hinobi Smash sg

Samara Thomas
Grade 7
NPS International School
Hillside Drive, Singapore

S am sat in front of the screen; his eyes glued to the action unfolding before him. His fingers flew across the keyboard and mouse, clicking and typing with lightning speed as he navigated through the virtual world. The room was dark and quiet, the only sound coming from the soft glow of the computer screen. The gamer sat in front of it, his eyes fixed on the action unfolding before him. His fingers moved quickly and confidently across the keyboard; his mind consumed by the game.

The hours ticked by as Sam played, lost in the virtual world and

the rush of adrenaline that came with each victory. He was completely absorbed in the game, his body tens and his mind focused with each task at hand. As the night wore on, Sam was unable to pull himself away, drawn back again and again by the allure of the virtual world and the endless cycle of winning and losing. His eyelids grew heavier and heavier until he couldn't keep them open anymore. 'Just a short nap' he thought to himself as he dozed off on his desk.

The next morning, he was woken up by his mum shaking him vigorously. His eyes opened and he saw his mum standing over him with an envelope in her hands. "What's in the envelope?" he asked groggily. "Why don't you open it and see for yourself?" his mum replied. Once he opened it, he read the letter inside which was addressed to him. As his eyes grew wide his mum asked, "What does it say?" "Hinobi, the company that made my favourite video game invited me to participate in a gaming championship!"

After hours of persuading his parents, Sam got permission to participate. He practiced day and night without fault until the day of the competition finally arrived. As he sat in the car with his parents, his heart pounded in his chest. "We've reached." His dad announced. He exited the car shaking like a leaf in the wind.

As he entered the building a woman stopped him and asked "Participant?" "Yeah, Sam Greens." he said. "Wear this" she replied passing him a bracelet. He took a deep breath and walked onto the platform where all the best players of Singapore assembled. "Hello participants." A loud voice boomed from the speakers "The championship will be a virtual reality scavenger hunt throughout Singapore! To win you must complete challenges and collect clues. The first person to reach the finish line wins the title of HINOBI SMASH CHAMPION! Activate your stations by tapping your bracelets on the code in front of you. The competition begins in 3, 2, 1 GO!!"

The next few hours whizzed by as Sam travelled speedily all over the country, clearing levels, collecting clues here and there. On his way to his first quest, he sped through the city and made his way to the Straits channel, one of the largest waterways in the entire country. An automated voice spoke through his headset 'Welcome player' it said 'The Strait channel is one of Singapore's most important waterways and is responsible for most of the imports to the country. In this quest, you will have to use the materials found around you to patch up the canal before it breaks, potentially causing floods and bringing harm to the citizens of Singapore.' Panicked, Sam whizzed around, looking for materials that he could use to fix the canal. Finally, he stumbled upon a large metal chunk. He picked up the large sheet, and flew towards the canal and patched it up, praying that it would stay put. 'Well done player.' The voice said 'You must now go to the Singapore skyline for your next and final quest. Good luck.'

Sam took a deep breath and prepared himself for the final part the challenge. He darted through the city, avoiding trees and double decker buses. Eventually, he reached the skyline of the city and gasped in awe. There was a line of buildings, taller than ones Sam had ever seen, and their lights illuminated the night sky. He was snapped out of his trance when a loud roar filled the air. He searched for the origin of the noise and found it, near the pearly white statue of the half-lion, half-fish creature named the Merlion. A large robot- like object was positioned at the foot of the statue. "To claim the title of Hinobi smash champion, you must first defeat me!" it said. After a heated battle between Sam and the bot, it crumbled and faded away making a teleporter. Sam headed towards it and tapped his bracelet on it. He was instantly brought back to the Hinobi building. "CONGRATULATIONS SAM GREENS FOR YOU ARE OFFICIALLY THE HINOBI SMASH CHAMPION!" the speaker boomed. One by one, all the other players emerged from the teleporter with disappointed looks on their faces, but Sam was overjoyed! He scanned the crowd for any sight of his parents and caught them waving wildly at him with grins plastered on their faces. When they went home, his mother told him "We are going to get you some better gaming devices. I saw you playing, and I was truly amazed. Well done Sam." As they headed to the gaming shop, Sam glanced at his gleaming, gold trophy smiling.

The Treasure

Tanatsiwa Christabel Dube
Grade 12
Gauteng, Johannesburg, South Africa

In the hush of uncertainty, Nomsa Ruponeso Nyathi's hands cradled the strange baby, and she questioned their differences. *Has there been a mistake?* Beside her, her husband, Brian Anderson, senses her unease. "What's on your mind?" he asks, and she responds cryptically with "Nothing." Brian sighs, understanding her uncertainty. Their car halts at the Cresta Oasis Hotel in Harare. Nomsa hands the baby to Brian. They were welcomed by Miss Khumalo, the receptionist, who noticed the child's unique appearance and frowns. Nomsa probes further, and Miss Khumalo hesitates before saying the baby seems "different." Nomsa's eyes well with tears. "What's wrong?" she inquires, her voice firm. "She's...different, but in a nice way, a cute bundle of joy," Miss Khumalo reassures. Yet, Nomsa's unease persisted.

She takes Courtney Atidaishe Anderson and leaves Brian to handle the interaction. Once in their suite, Nomsa places Courtney in a small white cot, her gaze reflecting a mix of wonder and concern. Moments later, she finds Brian busying himself with baby clothes. Nomsa musters the courage to speak. "Brian," she murmurs, "I think we should consider giving Courtney up for adoption." Brian glares at her. "Are you joking?" he retorted, immediately standing up. Nomsa averted his gaze. "Nomsa, she's our child," Brian reminds her, but she is absolute. "Brian, this child is different, and I can't even hold her. I thought I could, but I was wrong." Brian questioned her abrupt behaviour. Frustration simmered in his voice. Nomsa, walked away, avoiding confrontation and withdrew into solitude. Later that night, she is awakened by Courtney's cries. Reluctantly, she tended to the child, telling her to be quiet. Surprisingly, Courtney obeyed. Nomsa shrieked and called Brian, who concludes that she is delusional.

Morning arrived, and they stopped at a pit-stop near Norton. Nomsa saw an opportunity to abandon Courtney. She smiled, telling Brian she needed a few minutes to discard some items. In secret, she left Courtney's cot on a table and returned to the car. With a feeling of freedom, they returned home to Gweru. Nomsa is relieved, thinking she's finally escaped her burden. But as they enter their house, Brian's face darkens with anger. He demanded to know where Courtney is. Nomsa initially feigned ignorance but eventually admitted her heartless act, and Brian was livid. Their confrontation escalated, and Brian left the room, leaving Nomsa in guilt-ridden silence. Hours later, Nomsa approaches their bedroom. She found Brian clinging to a baby blanket, tears in his eyes. He's emotional as he told her, "You are the most important thing in my life, at least you were."

Nomsa's heart ached, realising the gravity of her actions.

Kunashe Katsande had been driving throughout the night, and his wife, Kudzai Chaderera, urged him to rest. He agreed, pulling into a pit-stop just after Norton. Kudzai settled in for a nap, and Kunashe took a moment to reflect. Life had treated Kunashe well. He had a loving wife, two bright daughters named Thandaza and Namatai, and a thirteen-year-old son named Atichengeta. Kunashe's success extended to his ownership of two sugar plantations in Triangle, while Kudzai was a successful founder of a multimillion-dollar networking business. Their strong Catholic faith bound them together through all of life's challenges. It seemed that their life couldn't get any better.

While Kunashe sipped on an energy drink, he heard a faint cry in the distance. He investigated and discovered a newborn baby girl abandoned in a carrier cot. A birth record with no name accompanied the baby. After soothing the baby and retrieving her belongings, Kunashe woke Kudzai and shared his discovery. They decided to keep the baby, and their journey home to Borrowdale, Harare, continued. At the Registrar General's office, they officially named the baby Savara Makatendeka Katsande. The attendant handed them a stamped birth certificate, making them Savara's legal parents. As they drove home, Kunashe and Kudzai marvelled at the baby's beauty and questioned why someone would abandon such a precious child.

Back home, their children Thandaza and Namatai welcomed the new addition to the family with excitement and joy. The Katsandes shared a moment of gratitude and love, knowing that Savara had brought them even closer together. In the evening, as the sun dipped below the horizon, the Katsande family gathered in their living room. Savara slept peacefully in Kudzai's arms, and the room was filled with a sense of contentment and love. Kunashe explained to his children the importance of valuing every life and treating others with kindness. As the night progressed, the Katsande family embraced the belief that love could turn discarded fragments into priceless treasures. They understood that every person had a unique story and the potential to shine brightly when given the chance.

Years passed, and Savara Makatendeka Katsande had established herself as a prominent and dedicated lawyer in Harare. Her reputation for championing justice and her unwavering commitment to making the world a better place was well-known. Her office was a sanctuary of legal texts, documents, and the comforting aroma of freshly brewed Tears streamed down Savara's cheeks as she nodded, her voice lost amidst the torrent of emotions. She stepped forward and embraced him, feeling the warmth of paternal love she had yearned for throughout those years. The years apart were now but a distant memory, replaced by an unbreakable bond that time and distance could never sever. In the ensuing weeks, Savara shared precious moments with her newfound sister and father. They pieced together fragments of their shared past while creating new memories for the future. In those quiet moments, she was happy to see her father's tired yet contented smile.

Indeed, one man's discarded treasure had become another's priceless gem, not just in terms of material possessions, but in the immeasurable value of relationships and the healing balm of love. Her journey, which had commenced with an abandoned baby on a cement table, had come full circle, illustrating that life's most profound lessons often emerge from the most unexpected corners. Standing at the crossroads of her past and present, Savara embraced the intricate beauty of life's tapestry, grateful for the lessons it had woven into her path.

My Dream Delivery man - A Dream path with the Gray Cloud

Seo-yeon, Oh
Grade 10, Uijeongbu girl's highschool
Uijeongbu, South Korea

I kept running on a wide field I'd never seen before. I ran with great energy, not feeling tired or resting. As I kept running like that, I could see the end. But as I approached it, a steep cliff was right in front of me. And a large cloud obscured my view. Unlike the bright white and subtly sky-blue clouds that were around me, the cloud was emitting a dark and strange gray color.

'Why is this cloud so ugly and unappealing?'

I was far away from the Seoul city now. I could not recognize the exact location too!

The gray cloud gradually approached me as soon as I was pondering it by myself. I tried to hold it with my hands, but I couldn't. Soon after, the cloud had eyes, a nose, and a mouth, and began to talk. I couldn't hear his voice clearly, but at first glance he seemed to be in pain. The gray cloud handed me something. It was a badge emblazoned with the words 'Dream'. The badge was almost broken, so it was difficult to identify the letter as well. The gray cloud held it in my hand and explained the situation to me easily.

Originally, he said he was one of the clouds working as a dream delivery man. He said that the process of delivering a dream takes ten years and more than seventeen years. Therefore, dream delivery men are told to choose only one person among the many people who will achieve their dreams. The gray cloud finally chose me after thinking and thinking about it for a long time.

Thus, when I entered elementary school, he started a dream delivery, and until I finished middle school, he was able to deliver more stably and faster than any cloud without any trouble.

However, after entering high school, when I gave up my dream and started to wander, problems began to occur in the delivery process of my dream. After nearly a year in that state, it came to a situation where dream delivery was no longer possible.

After hearing the story from the cloud, I became emotional and eventually began to shed tears. I didn't want to give up the dream I had held for that long time. I just tried to give up because I wasn't confident that I would go through the process of achieving my dream in the future.

The gray cloud that heard my story said that he fully understood how I felt, and promised to wait until I had a dream again like before.

I told the cloud, "I will not run away from now either. Although I have no dream and I am wandering a lot now, I will consider it also a precious process before I achieve my dream in the future. Thank you, gray cloud, for trusting and supporting me until the end.", attaching the dream badge to the left chest of the gray cloud. Then, the dream badge slowly began to glow red, and the gray cloud no longer emitted gray light, turning into a white cloud more beautiful and dazzling than any other cloud around it. The gray cloud held my hand and began to scream, running together on the vast field I had been running on.

"Seo-yeon, we're starting again now, I'll guide you on the path of your dreams, so you bloom your dreams!" I smiled, nodding towards the gray cloud.

Saying goodbye like that, the dream delivery man disappeared, and I woke up from my dream. Even though it was a dream, I came to believe that my dream delivery man was always by my side. "My dream delivery man, you are still watching me from the sky, right? Wait a minute, the day we meet again, I will tell you all night about my dreams."

I feel like something good is going to happen to me today.

Everyone's Fence

Cesar Esteve
Grade 5
Nuestra Señora Consolacion School
Villacañas, Toledo, Spain

In our school, we have been working as a team for a long time. Our teachers tell us that we are the protagonists of our learning and that we must never stop feeling, dreaming, imagining, acting and sharing. The students at my school, called Ntra. 'Señora de la Consolación' loves to participate in many projects, especially in projects where we, the students, can participate and design changes in our town. It is fascinating!

I am going to tell you a wonderful story that happened thanks to the creativity of the students at the school. One day in Don Sergio's class, our teacher told us what the I CAN methodology consisted of and how we could carry it out in the village. He encouraged all the students to move around the village looking for places that we could improve. We called the project "Know your town, live safely" and we set off, so that what started as a proposal would finally become a reality.

Everything happened because we wanted that on May 1st, in our most nationally known festival called: "El Cristo de la Viga y sus danzantes", the people could feel safe throughout the three days of the festival. In this festival, the people enjoy the processions in the streets where the Christ is accompanied by eight dancers who dance and sing nonstop. The students at the school Ntra. de la Consolación decided to make a project so that the town could enjoy more of this celebration. We thought of a lot of ideas, one of these ideas was to create a fence, next to the nursery school, since the procession and the dancers were going to pass through there and we knew that this place should be safer since many young children pass through there with their grandparents. We thought of designing a fence there because it could save many lives since it would serve to protect the children who were near the park, the kindergarten and the school that is nearby.

Everything went as follows:

From April 27 to May 1 on the occasion of the festivities in our town, there was a very beautiful procession where the "El Cristo de la Viga" went, which is so called because during a storm at sea a ship was sinking and in the beam of the ship a Christ appeared to them and saved the eight sailors from drowning. Since then, every year we remember this miracle and the whole town enjoys the festivities. But one day during the festivities, a mother went to take her son to the nursery school as a normal day basically, but when she returned to pick him up, she did not see him, because there were many people enjoying the procession. When she couldn't find him, all the students from the school, worked as a team and helped the police to look for him. In the end, we found him. He was playing in the park, but again due to the crowds, we lost sight of him. Then we saw the boy running into the street because he wanted to go dancing with one of the dancers. Luckily the fence, which the students at the school thought of and designed, did a great job, due to which it was impossible for the boy to leave the yard. The boy seemed to have given up, but again he ran out and saw a gap between two bars and tried to squeeze through, but the fence was very strong, and he couldn't get through. The fence was also very narrow, so he started to give up and while waiting for his mom to come and pick him up, he started to entertain himself by counting the colors of that majestic fence. By the time his mother finally managed to reach her son, our intrepid protagonist was dancing to the rhythm of the wind and the songs sung by the dancers.

Once the town festival was over, the mayor of Villacañas and the dancers thanked us for having helped the police look for the child and told us that he wanted to give us a gift to the school for our nice deed. Together, all the students at the school decided to help us to collect the food of our town: pistachios, grapes, pisto manchego, cheese, porridge and donuts, to give it to the poor children in Spain and the rest of the world. Thanks to this idea, children from all over the world were able to taste our typical products and get to know our wonderful town and our popular festival.

Through the Lens of a Dream

Thisun Kovida
Grade 11
De Mazenod College
Kandana, Sri Lanka

Kevin was walking along the lonely winding road. It was a gloomy morning with a drizzle of rain. He was half wet, but he didn't mind; he had more pressing problems in mind. Making no effort to quicken his pace as the rain pelted down harder, he walked slower still to a rather crowded road where school children were rushing inside to get out of the rain. He was at school: the place that had become a living hell for him.

He reflected upon the past when he used to enjoy school. After his father's new promotion, his whole family was uprooted from their old home and onto a completely new setting. All his protests and sulking were met with adults' reasoning. The transition from the busy city to the quieter and lonely town didn't agree with him. He had left behind his friends, school, and life.

The only reminder of his past was the faithful camera that still kept him company. He could remember the first time he had had a chance to touch a camera. He was six when his great-uncle visited them from America. He had a small camera in his vast amount of baggage. Kevin had been curiously exploring some of it when he came across this strange machine that he had never seen before. His great-uncle had found him and had kept Kevin on his knee as he showed him how to take a picture. Kevin was so mesmerized that his uncle had let him keep it. Since that day, photography had become Kevin's passion, his mentor, and pretty much his whole life. He had dedicated himself to mastering the art of photography. His unique talent, enthusiasm, and hard work had earned him the role of president of the Photography Unit at his previous school.

Kevin stood idly, his eyes out of focus as he reminisced on these thoughts. He was brought back to his senses by an urgent voice.

"Kev, what are you doing?"

He turned abruptly but he was face-to-face with his best friend, his only solace in this dreadful place. Jason's company was the only thing that helped him survive this place. They were in the same class and both introverts clicked together at once.

"Get inside. Are you dreaming? You're already wet!" continued Jason.

"Oh well! If we must," replied Kevin with contempt. He had always been insolent, yet he could not disregard his only friend completely.

They paused at the noticeboard to find a bright poster inviting young photographers to submit their creations to *"Photo Fiesta: Lens Legends Battle 2023."* Both friends stared at this new notice for a full minute before looking excitedly at each other. Kevin knew that this was his chance; he had always been interested in photography, and Jason was a master of painting. He undoubtedly knew the beauty and worth of a good picture.

For the first time, Kevin found this school fascinating, inviting even. There was something that mattered to him in this place. The thought was overwhelming. Suddenly, "Photo Fiesta" became the sole topic of conversation among the two friends. They got their hands on application forms from the school office and got to work. After school, the two friends met up to brainstorm ideas for their captures. They considered natural landscapes, historical buildings, street scenes, and wildlife. Kevin's photography background proved to be a valuable asset.

Their afternoons were spent exploring the Kandana town, scouting for picturesque locations and interesting subjects. Kandana is a suburb of Colombo in Western Province, Sri Lanka, 19 km north of the Colombo city centre. Due to the proximity to Colombo, Negombo as well as the Bandaranaike International Airport, the suburb is a popular and beautiful residential area.

Armed with Kevin's camera and Jason's keen eye for composition, they captured the beauty of the Kandana that had once felt so distant to Kevin. Through this newfound ambition to win the contest, they embarked upon something much more valuable than a mere material treasure. Their friendship deepened as Kevin bonded with the town in all those afternoons and in the evenings when they ventured inside the forest in the hope of finding new subject material. Jason, with his sketchbook in hand, captured the same scene from a different perspective, blending his artistic talent with Kevin's photography skills.

This awesome project not only heightened their friendship but also allowed Kevin to find a sense of belonging in his new environment. The day of submission arrived, and they carefully packaged their entries. Their hearts pounded with excitement mingled with nervousness as they handed in their creations to the contest organizers. Regardless of the outcome, they knew they had learned so much through their evenings together.

"Participation is the true prize" they reminded themselves. Yet, they were keen for the results to come in. Lately, though introverts, Jason and Kevin seemed to have caught the attention of the whole school. Their pictures were admired by both teachers and students alike. It was as if their talents had been hidden for far too long, and now they were finally being recognized. People couldn't stop talking about how amazing their work was.

After a fortnight of anticipation, the results were finally released. Amazingly, Jason and Kevin had won the grand prize! Jason, who got the news first, ran up to Kevin's and banged on his door until Kevin opened the door, his eyes half shut.

"What's going on, Jason? It's Saturday! Can't I sleep in peace even on the weekend?"

"Well, would you rather sleep than hear this news? I warn you; you'll regret it."

"Never mind, I'm already up. What's the hurry about?"

"WE WON THE GRAND PRIZE!"

Words couldn't express Kevin's delight. For a whole week, they were the talk of the town. As the grand prize winners, their work was prominently featured in a photography exhibition held in their town. Moreover, they became mentors to the budding photographers who were trying to capture the beauty of life through a lens.

Their success served as a nostalgic reminder that life's greatest treasures are often found in the pursuit of one's passions and in the bonds of true friendship. It was a lesson that they carried with them throughout their lives, a reminder that, in the end, it was not the destination but the path they took that truly mattered.

Echoes of the Past

**Nagwan Ahmed Abdelrahim
Elhagmustafa
Grade 10
British Educational Institute
Khartoum, Sudan**

O nce upon a time, in the heart of Africa, there lay a country called Sudan. Her history was rich, painted with vibrant hues of culture, tradition, and unity. Families gathered under the shade of acacia trees, sharing tales of ancestors who roamed the vast savannahs, and children played freely in the golden fields, their laughter echoing through the valleys.

As the sun dipped below the horizon, the rhythm of drums filled the air, accompanied by the melodious chants of singers paying homage to their land. The pinnacle of diversity. Tribes coexisted in harmony, celebrating each other's differences as threads that wove together the fabric of their nation.

But alas, the winds of change began to blow, carrying with them the seeds of discord and strife. Political tensions simmered, and lines were drawn in the sand, dividing communities once bound by kinship. Sounds of gunfire replaced the melodies of old.

Families fled their homes, seeking refuge from the storm that swept across the land. The laughter of children was silenced, replaced by the cries of anguish and fear. The country's bright future dimmed under the shadow of war, leaving behind a trail of broken dreams and shattered hopes.

I, too, had to leave my home behind.

Yet, amidst the chaos and despair, a small flicker of resilience remained. Communities silently banded together, drawing strength from the bonds forged in hardship. They refused to let the darkness extinguish the light that still burned within their hearts. My people still dared to dream of a brighter tomorrow.

I watched, for the last time, as the sun rose over the horizon, casting its golden rays upon the land. Sudan stood on the threshold of a new era. Though scarred by the trials of time, it somehow remained a beacon of hope, a testament to the unbreakable spirit of my people.

Gathering what little we could carry, me and my family embarked on a journey into the unknown, leaving behind the familiar landscapes and cherished memories that had defined our lives for generations. Bloodshed in the streets that had once been my home. I could no longer remain here. My only home is now a battlefield.

Each step we took was heavy with the weight of sorrow and loss as we traversed desolate roads and crossed treacherous borders, the shadows of our past trailed behind us like ghosts in the night. I watched as the landscape transformed, the colours of my land fading into the bleak monotony of exile. I kept wondering if we could rebuild what had been lost and carve out a new life from the ashes of the old.

Though the distance stretched out before us like an endless abyss, I held fast to the memories of Sudan, carrying them like a beacon of light to guide me through the darkest of nights. For even as I left behind the land of my birth, its spirit remained etched upon my soul, a testament to the enduring strength of the human spirit in the face of adversity.

Dar-es-Salaam

Ria Susan Jijo
Grade 10
Aga Khan Secondary School
Dar-es-Salaam, Tanzania

It is a bright and sunny evening. The sun's rays blaze down from the sky and I decide to watch the sunset at the beach. I get into my car and soon arrive at a semi-crowded coastline. Tranquility and bliss cover me in a warm embrace. The sand tickles my toes and the waves wash over them in swift, graceful movements. The gentle ocean breeze carries a salty smell, wafting into my nostrils with the aroma of fried fish, hot chips and roasted peanuts. The atmosphere is melodious: the steady rhythm of lapping waves, the whispers of the palm trees swaying and the energetic beats of Swahili songs create a discordant jazz song. The sun has almost set, so I grab my packet of peanuts and walk back to my car.

As I drive along the coast, back to the main city, I glance up and look at the cauldron of bats swirling overhead – their screeches and flapping of wings, a muted background sound to the hubbub of the city. The traffic light turns a bright red. Cars are honking, people talking, blinking streetlights, and hawkers – so many hawkers – covering every window of the car, pulling up every item imaginable for sale: toys, stationery, mirrors, brushes and house decorations. Two young boys appear with a makeshift container containing soapy water and cleaning clothes. They pour the water on my windshield and meticulously scrub and wipe until it is sparkly clean – their way of making money. The light turns green and I keep driving.

I decide to visit the Cathedral and pull over into the beautiful compound. I park my car and stand outside, marveling at the large structure. The towering cathedral's smooth grey-and-white walls stand strong and proud, diligently observing the arriving vehicles.

"Roho yangu na ikuimbie, Jinsi wewe ulivyo mkuu..." (Then sings my soul, my Saviour God, to Thee, How great Thou art, How great Thou art...)

The powerful singing of hymns in the cathedral with the steady rhythm of drums jolts me from my trance, and I walk up the stairs into the beautiful church. The glass-stained walls and the high ceilings create a majestic cove that carries the echo of the singing. The choir singers are dressed in vivid shades of traditional Kitenge dresses; some wear distinct Kitenge head wraps, and others are adorned with colourful, beaded jewellery. Their voices are loud and clear, and their graceful movements are in time to the music. I sit there and listen, truly mesmerized and recollecting all the childhood memories I spent at this church; I remember sitting at the front pews of the church, singing the church out of sorrow but out of gratitude for the good life I was able to live.). She thanks me for my help and tells me it was nice to talk to me. I respond with a final greeting and part ways with her.

I understood that this city had helped her to live happily with its beauty and tradition. On my way home, I stop at one of my favourite local food outlets. I get confused about whether to buy the delicious barbeque chicken, the nyama choma beef, or the chipsmayayi. I wave at the friendly owner and order one chipsmayayi, a wonderful delicacy with eggs and chips.

"Asante sana[1]!" I say in gratitude as he serves my meal, handing him the crisp Tanzanian shilling notes.

"Karibu tena[2]" he replied. "Next time, try the Nyama Choma[3] as well!"

Dar-es-Salaam is distinguished by its fine restaurants, lively nightlife, and many beautiful beaches. Its status as the economic center of Tanzania is well-connected to the surrounding cities, Zanzibar[4] and the national parks to the south. I often feel that the city ranks as high in beauty in the minds of Tanzanians as Kilimanjaro.

I grin and finish the plate in record time. As I drive home, I look back at the bustling city lights and admire the amazing culture, energy, and beauty of Dar-es-Salaam. This city - my first home – will always have a special place in my heart.

---

1 *Asante sana: Thank you*

2 *Karibu tena: Welcome*

3 *Nyama choma beef: A traditional and popular roasted meat in Tanzania and Kenya*

4 *Zanzibar: A Tanzanian archipelago off the coast of East Africa.*

Loy Krathong - The Festival of Light

Punyawatt
Grade10
Assumption College Sriracha
Thailand

Pal, a backpacker with a deep love for nature, arrived in Thailand brimming with excitement. He'd heard whispers of Loy Krathong[1], the festival of lights, and pictured a magical night filled with flickering candles dancing on water. But as the day approached, his conversations with friendly shopkeepers painted a different picture.

"The river gets choked with plastic after Loy Krathong," said Anika, a woman selling woven baskets. "Even the natural ones take ages to decompose." Pal's heart sank. Images of beautiful waterways clogged with garbage replaced his vision of glowing candles.

Later, chatting with a tuk-tuk driver named Somchai, Pal learned more. "Some people put fireworks in their krathongs," Somchai explained, shaking his head. "Scares the fish and birds something fierce." Pal winced, picturing panicked wildlife fleeing the sudden bursts of light and noise.

The night of Loy Krathong arrived, and the town shimmered with an ethereal beauty. Pal, torn between the spectacle and his growing concern, decided to explore. He saw families setting their decorated krathongs adrift, their faces reflecting the warm glow of candlelight. It was undeniably beautiful.

But then, he spotted a clogged canal, its surface littered with soggy remnants of krathongs. A pang of sadness hit him. This beautiful tradition, he realized, was having a negative impact on the environment he cherished.

---

1 *Loy Krathong: festival celebrated annually throughout Thailand*

Back at his hostel, Pal bumped into a group of Thai university students. They were organizing a campaign for eco-friendly Loy Krathong celebrations. They used bread dough and leaves to make the krathongs and collected them after the festival for composting.

Relief washed over Pal. There was a way to celebrate while protecting the environment! He joined their efforts, helping spread awareness and teaching tourists about sustainable alternatives.

Loy Krathong became a turning point for Pal. He realized that cultural traditions, however beautiful, needed to adapt to a changing world. He left Thailand determined to be a responsible traveler, promoting eco-conscious practices wherever he went.

One of them

Deniz Yavaş
Grade 12
TED Bodrum College
Bodrum, Turkey

I onia is in the Aegean Region of today. It has hosted many civilizations throughout history, witnessed many historical events, and brought most of history to the present day. Herodotus, the father of history, defined the Ionia of history as follows:

"The Ionians founded their cities under the most beautiful sky and in the most beautiful climate we know on earth. Neither the regions further north nor those further south can be equated with Ionia; even neither east nor west. Some are cold and wet; some are hot and dry."

And undoubtedly, the most fascinating land of Ionia is Halicarnassus.

Yaşar was born in this fascinating land, and as he got older, he began to understand and live in Bodrum. In Bodrum, olive picking started at the end of November, but it was never called harvest. The topic was neighbors; children would go to olive groves. First mine, then yours... Meals were cooked at home so that they could be eaten while the olives were picked at noon. It was a tradition; old people were tired, and children were happy. It would be a game for them. Thanks were always given to those who left, those who planted and grew...

Yaşar has also grown up now. Even though his little hands were freezing in the cold, he would collect these golden grains one by one from the grass. Of course, sometimes thorns were unavoidable. But okay! The cure was again in the fruit of this miracle tree. With a little olive oil, all Yaşar's pain would go away.

It was school, student life, military service, and years passed. Yaşar had studied. Otherwise, he would either become a fisherman or a sponge diver and spend his years at sea and not be able to earn his living. In the July heat of 1981, he completed his final preparations and threw himself into the dark blue sea, with the tube on his back and the flippers on his feet...

Years ago, when describing Bodrum, it was described as a paradise of eternal blues. Most parts of the peninsula have that view, endless blue. Those blue fields take people to other lands. He brought some of them to the present day with their ruins...

The Aslan Burnu wreck was 30 meters deep. As they approached the target, the sarcophagi would escape into the broken amphoras. He lived and found the healthy ones left in between. This is what all his work for years was about. Divers would remove the amphoras carefully and properly. Yaşar was one of them. The amphoras he unearthed looked familiar to him. He had seen their pictures many times at school. They were gum amphoras. They examined them carefully in Bodrum Castle. Nearly 2500 olive seeds were found inside one of them. This amphora belonged to 400 BC. Therefore, they thought that the olive pits were the history that the sea had brought to the present day...

Maybe Herodotus, the Father of History, used these olives, Yaşar thought. Maybe he used their oil, maybe he used them himself. Who knows, Herodotus left the ship of the merchant who escaped from what storm and took shelter in Halicarnassus, and dived into the eternal blue while sipping the famous wine mixed with seawater.

Tourism was just beginning in those years. Bodrum even had a nursery rhyme:

"Bodrum Bodrum... Two shops and one furnace, there is no mouth or nose left to eat cheese and bread!"

In the Bodrum dialect, the oven was called "furun". But Bodrum was happy. It was very attached to its past. It even drank its water from the Salmakis fountain described by Strabo. This fountain took its name from Peri Salmakis. Salmakis fell in love with Aphrodite's son and prayed to the gods who loved Halicarnassus to bring them together in one body. Bodrum residents used to drink water from this fountain for 12 months. Yaşar also used to go to the fountain frequently. After all, he was a Bodrum resident who loved his country and its history...

Yaşar was also interested in fishing. From time to time, he would even try to raise the small mullet he caught by scattering them in the large concrete pool in the tangerine garden. His grandmother used to cook beans, Yaşar's favorite dish, over the fire of tangerine wood in these tangerine gardens, in earthenware pots called Çukale. Yaşar used to say that it was very delicious. We've all done it when we were in primary school. A bean grain was taken, wrapped in damp cotton, and after it sprouted, it was brought into the soil...

Since Yaşar was from Gümüşlük, he knew Asar Island. Jumping off the back of the island was a sign of bravery when they were children. This island was later named Rabbit Island. Because Grandpa Arif released rabbits onto the island. This island was in the middle of the blue that they call eternal. The view was also great. The top of the island overlooked the Myndos harbour. From there, one would once again go back to the past with blue skies...

Myndos was also a historical city that hosted many people in its time. Myndos, where Caesar's murderer Brutus hid for 2 years... Myndos, where Alexander anchored his fleet... Myndos, which changed the belief that beans came to Anatolia from South America in the

17th century and proved that beans were eaten by cooking them in a clay pot, just like Yaşar ate them years ago. ... Perhaps Herodotus, Hippocrates, Queen Ada and many others have tasted the same beans. Maybe they got a taste of the same Halicarnassus...

Maybe they had tasted the same Halicarnassus. Maybe Yaşar had also tasted the Bodrum he fell in love with. However, Bodrum would host many more Yaşars who needed to see this fascinating city, drink this water, pick tangerines from the trees, taste these beans, and want to be caught up in the magic of Myndos... So, what would be left for them?

History is covered by the soil, the concrete piles with which we destroyed the soil!

A Holiday Trip

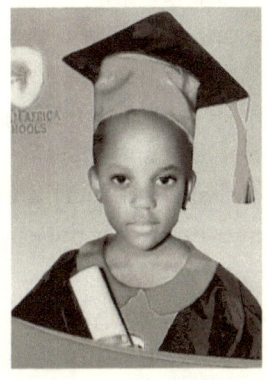

Shahnaz Fadalla Ibrahim
Grade 3
Dream Africa School
Makindye, Kampala, Uganda

My name is Namasi, and I'm studying in grade 5. We decided to go on a tour during my vacation as we had planned. When I put this request to my father, he agreed and decided to visit our grandparents' village and the nearby Nile River.

So, on the first Sunday of my vacation, we set off to see the village in eastern Uganda where my grandparents live. Father drove the car. Mom sat in the front seat with my younger sister Amira on her lap. My elder brother Akunda and I were in the back seat with the things we had bought to give to our grandparents.

The day went as desired near the village in Jinja, the source of the Nile River and Lake Victoria, Africa's largest lake. My father had arranged a village tour in the car before reaching our grandparents. I was very happy to see the sights which were so different from the hustle and bustle of the city.

My father told me that Jinja was a town on the shores of Lake Victoria in Southern Uganda. My mother proudly added that this is the source of the Nile River. We saw Owen Falls Dam and Bujagali Dam spanning the Nile. On the north side of the river, when I mentioned Itanda Falls, which is famous for its waterfalls, I really wanted to visit there, but Dad said it could be another time when we were visiting Grandpa and Grandma. Samuka Island, located east of Jinja in Lake Victoria, is home to birdlife, including the little egret, and I didn't object when my father told me we could go there next holiday.

Grandfather and grandmother were delighted to see the Nile passing by not far from where they lived. Once we reached my grandparents, I ran to them. Jajja picked me up and kissed me. In our tradition, we call grandparents "Jajja".

Near my grandfather's house, I saw many varieties of jackfruit, avocado, and many other fruits. The day after we arrived, my brother Akunda and Uncle Papijo, who were on vacation, taught me how to climb trees and swing on a mapera (Guava tree). That evening, grandfather went to the fishing ground near the Nile and bought a big fish for lunch, and we enjoyed a delicious dinner of fish and matoke.

As we walked through the village, we had a chance to meet and talk to many people. Coming from the hustle and bustle of the city, everything was new and joyful for me and my brother. We felt that our relatives and others were also very happy as they were seeing us after a long time. The official languages of Uganda are Swahili and English. But I realized that people in the village mostly speak Swahili.

I was overjoyed to see the Nile so close. My grandpa explained about its specialty and how this river had helped the African land for thousands of years. He taught me the history and culture of the country and how the river Nile was linked with them.

My grandfather said that the Nile River is a great asset to our land as it provides a source of irrigation to transform the surrounding arid area into rich agricultural land. Today, it is understood that the river serves not only as a source of irrigation but also as an important transport and trade route.

During our stay, my grandmother taught us how to pick coffee from the trees, and brother Akunda taught us how to fish using hooks and fishing baskets in the Nile where the water was not deep. At night near the fire, grandmother sang local songs, and we danced Baganda dances. My small sister Amira danced very well, and Jaja gave her a big hen for winning the dance competition.

Before we traveled back to Kampala, Dad's brother took us to the river, and we waited with him while he caught three big fish and roasted them for us using firewood. We ate two fish, and we brought one big fish back home. Also, grandmother packed soya beans, avocados, and sweet potatoes. We enjoyed our holidays very much. We came back very happy.

On our way back to Kampala, we visited Lake Victoria. Armed

with textbook knowledge, I curiously inquired about Lake Victoria from my father. My father explained to me about Lake Victoria and

the city of Kampala. It was the most interesting thing I've ever heard.

Dad said that Lake Victoria borders the city of Kampala, Uganda's national commercial capital, an urban center of red-tiled villas, hills covered with trees, and contemporary skyscrapers. In the downtown area, the Uganda Museum explores the country's tribal heritage through its extensive collection of artifacts.

After enjoying the night view of Lake Victoria, we returned to our home in Kampala. And so, a happy holiday trip made us all happy. Most of the shops were seen closed. By the time we reached the heart of Kampala city, it was late at night. The city was almost covered in darkness. We all laughed when Dad joked that just like us, the city too was tired and going to sleep after its non-stop run.

As the car drove down the narrow road to where our flat stood, I noticed some children roaming nearby on the footpath so late into the night! On closer observation, I realized that some of them were my age. When I asked why they were still on the street, my dad said that it was because they don't have a home to stay in. It was a shock for me, and I was saddened to hear that.

That sight made me realize that not everyone has the same facilities as us. Although the joy of the day's journey faded with the view in the city that night, I felt that it infused something else into me...

Wings in the Sky

Saeed Ali
Grade 8
Military School, Sharjah
United Arab Emirates.

Ali is a young Emirati boy. This young boy always inquired about the tradition and culture amidst the golden sands and endless skies of the United Arab Emirates because he was a student at the Military School, where the echoes of tradition and duty resonated through the corridors of his life.

From the moment he could comprehend, Ali was instilled with the values of honoring his country and its rich history. With a lineage steeped in military service, patriotism coursed through his veins like a silent anthem. Every day, as he donned his crisp uniform and made his way to school, a sense of pride and purpose enveloped him.

It wasn't merely the rigorous military training that shaped Ali; it was the vast expanse of the desert that surrounded his school. Amidst the endless dunes, where the only companions were the shifting sands and the boundless sky, Ali found solace and inspiration. Here, he felt as though he could conjure a new world with just his imagination.

One fateful day, while wandering in the desert, Ali witnessed a majestic falcon soaring through the azure heavens. Its wings spread wide, slicing through the air with grace and freedom. At that moment, an idea took flight within Ali's mind—a story waiting to be told.

Armed with nothing but his pen and unwavering determination, Ali embarked on a journey across the seven emirates, seeking inspiration to pen down a story from the rich culture of his homeland. With his father by his side, he explored the historical wonders that dotted the landscape, each site steeped in culture and tradition. Ali's father served as his guide.

During the visit to the historical places, Ali listened intently as his father recounted tales passed down through generations, each narrative weaving a spellbinding tapestry of history and myth. Ali's father elucidated that handicraft manufacturing helps the economic importance of the country and how these crafts serve as a vital source of income, particularly for smaller villages. He realized how the traditional storytelling, nomadic lyrics, and the Bedouin vernacular held a revered place in the hearts of its people. Amidst the rhythmic beats of traditional music, such as the "hudā" and traditional dances like "ayyālah," Ali felt the pulse of his homeland. Originating from caravanners traversing the desert trails, these melodies resonated with the spirit of resilience and wanderlust. All these graceful movements led him to a testament to the unity and pride of the Emirati people.

Ali's father acted as a beacon of wisdom by weaving tales of heritage and legacy. He enlightened Ali on the significance of each cultural facet they encountered. Ali realized that pottery, weaving, and metalworking are all integral to the cultural fabric of his nation. Each lesson learned along their journey illuminated the path forward, inspiring Ali to embrace his roots with pride and reverence.

Throughout their journey, Ali came to realize that much like other countries in the Arabian Peninsula, the United Arab Emirates boasted a rich tradition of traditional arts and cultural practices. Amidst the bustling souks and ancient fortresses, Ali found himself yearning for freedom, much like the falcon that had sparked his imagination. And thus, in his story, he imbued the lessons learned from his military schoolteachers, such as the values of bravery, loyalty, and resilience, as well as the knowledge he gained from his travel to historical places.

As the sun dipped below the horizon, casting a warm glow upon the desert, Ali reflected on his journey. He realized that honoring his country and its traditions was not merely a duty but a privilege—one he vowed to uphold with every fiber of his being. With each stroke of his pen, Ali felt a sense of pride knowing that his story is not only a symbol of the indomitable spirit that coursed through the veins of his people but also has the power to inspire others. And so, as the stars illuminated the night sky above the Burj Khalifa, Ali made a silent promise to continue his quest, to soar higher than ever before, just like the falcon that graced the heavens with its graceful flight.

The Long Road Home

Siddharth Menon
Grade 11
GEMS Modern Academy
Dubai, United Arab Emirates.

Sitting reclined on cushions that feel like pieces of clouds, I take in the picturesque view from the air-conditioned confines of my room. My eyes drift over the endless carpet of manicured green surrounding the Mansoori Mansion nestled in an uptown neighbourhood in the heart of Dubai; bejewelled with the gardener's choice of flowering plants that play with the gentle breeze and warm sunlight, inviting bees and birds to make it their home. Far beyond the gates, the bright blue sky is ornamented with shimmering skyscrapers, dominated by the Burj Khalifa, that stands like a lighthouse steering dreamers who have lost their way into a safe harbour of belief that dreams can be envisioned and made to come true. Would anyone believe that this land was once just a desert?

The playful giggles of one of my grandchildren take me back to that hot summer afternoon when I landed on the shores of Port Rashid on a cargo ship with Rs. 1000 in my pocket and a bag full of dreams, as just Sulaiman. With no friend or relative to help me in a strange land that lay across the seas, I had bid my family in India farewell to "the Gulf" with courage that flows only in the boiling blood of youth. I had weathered difficulty, uncertainty, and heat to build the empire that I now have, one milestone at a time.

Today, I have seen it all, every one of my dreams realized.

I am Sulaiman Al Mansouri, founder of Mansouri Group of Industries. The newspapers once called me Middle East's Raging Business Tycoon whose wealth and name were a result of shrewd business acumen and spirited dedication. I smile at the play of words and remember how my mother's prayers, the goodwill of friends and oftentimes strangers, luck and hard work had steered me into the path that made me a successful businessman. Today, I have built my empire, a loving family, and a big circle of friends. As head of the family, I have been given the biggest room in the Mansoori Mansion with the best view as I spend day after day in the confines of my air-conditioned palace, watching the world race by - a world I no longer seem to be a part of. Oftentimes my thoughts drift back to the bygone days, and I remember my friends who stood by me through thick and thin and have now secured a place in their heavenly abode, while I await my turn.

"Good morning, Baba," exclaims my oldest, Rashid, bringing me back to the present. I look at him and see not the little child who held my hand but a leader who shares the reins of an empire along with his twin sister, Alisha, the shy little girl who has grown into becoming the strong and confident businesswoman, who makes a loud appearance soon after him.

"And today we are going to the beach, and breakfast at Uncle Raed's," she exclaims, planting a kiss on my wrinkled cheek. My lips twitch in a smile of acceptance as my thoughts fill with memories of my friend Raed whose cafeteria was where I met clients, struck deals, and made connections that anchored me into the business world. The idea of returning there, in my current state, seems like one of life's ironies. As Alisha steers my electric wheelchair towards the car, my longing for the freedom I once knew overpowers my worries.

I sit a silent spectator as they drive through the city. I cannot help but marvel at how Dubai has evolved since my prime, a testament to the relentless progress of time. As we approach the beach, the briny aroma of the sea wafts through a slit in the window. I feel a renewed sense of anticipation. Rashid skilfully navigates the wheelchair across the sandy terrain until we reach the water's edge, while I notice that all of Alisha's skills do not curtail the excitement of my grandchildren thrilled at the sight of water.

The sight before us is breathtaking. The blue Arabian Gulf stretches out endlessly, its azure waters glistening in the brilliant sunlight. The vibrant sounds of laughter from children and the distant chatter of beachgoers compose a symphony of life.

I close my eyes. I hear the rhythmic lullaby of the tides and feel it. The sky above, the golden sand below and peace within. I feel one with

the universe. I savour the sensation of the gentle caress of the sun onto my aging face. It is as if time has rewound, and I am once again a free man, unburdened by the weight of my illness. I whisper a heartfelt thank you in the direction of the heavens, reminding myself that no matter how rich or powerful a person is, the greatest treasures of life are the ones that can never be bought but experienced - the freedom to enjoy the sunset, the laughter of the children and tranquility of the sea. As the waves caress the shores, I am just Sulaiman once again, embarking on my final journey that seems uncertain, but sure.

Brushstrokes

Daryl Jane Bukelo
Grade 9
GEMS Modern Academy
Dubai, United Arab Emirates

I used to have a twin brother. He used to come here with me every month, to Al Qudra Lake. It feels so long ago; now I stand here alone, looking at the clear, running water, its gentle gurgling soothing me. I see the sun as it shines on my face, peeking through the branches.

With peaceful beaches to lounge on, bustling boulevards to stroll in, and an abundance of al fresco attractions, there are plenty of ways to enjoy a sunny day in Dubai. Those seeking more tranquil scenery, however, will find it at Al Qudra Lakes! Al Qudra is an artificial oasis in Dubai. This popular eco-tourism destination is ideal for wildlife watchers and those seeking to reconnect with nature. This zone is the Al Marmoom Desert Conservation Reserve.

I set down an easel, bring out my acrylics, and pick a bird to paint. It's a crowned crane. It snatches my attention with its high-and-mighty stature, and for a moment, I am in a trance, gazing as it strides to the bank and fluffs its feathers. I know this because my brother was a nature enthusiast. The sound of the birds fills my mind as I lay out the sketch, reminding me of the days he would insist on me coming to paint with him here. I start to squeeze out the colors, remembering the memories on this shore. I squeeze so hard that my knuckles turn white.

I start to paint, forgetting about everything else. The serenity washes over me, and I see people look at me curiously and walk past. But soon, there is no one, and I don't know how long I stand there and paint, each brushstroke meeting the canvas to recreate the bird the way I see it. One after the other, the strokes meet, and I start to see the image, slowly but surely. I am immersed in the technique; the paint glides over the sketch as if it knows where to go. The colors mix and blend like scientific magic, and the brush is my ally. I lose track of time so easily—and when I am painting, nothing else matters. I came here to paint for a competition, and the theme was nature, so I knew I had to try.

I step back for a moment and look. It's good. But the more I look, the more I see that something is missing, and I don't know what. After all, the painting is just a bird.

I walk over to the banks myself, wetting my shoes. I bend over to touch the cold water, and I see little fish swimming about, without a care in the world. I fix my gaze on one tiny fish, watching it wriggle about in the water, circling my finger. There is some bread that I take out of my bag, and I feed it to the birds, whispering to them, asking them what I should add to my painting. They look at me through their beady eyes, with listless, timid expressions, their little heads bobbing to and from as they come to eat from my hand and listen to my inane monologues.

That's when I hear a noise.

I glance at the bushes next to me. It is silent for a while, but I see them slightly shudder with movement, and at first, I think I am looking at a mirror; but my eyes focus, and I realize what I am seeing.

My hands loosen, and the paintbrush falls on the soil. My heart is in my mouth as if bringing back all the grief I had swallowed for so long. Paint smudges on the muddy ground, but it doesn't matter; I run to the bushes, stumbling as I sprint, keeping my eyes fixed as if the vision is going to disappear if I blink. "THEO!" I shout, and my voice does not sound like my own.

He is not there, and I crumble to the ground. My eyes scan the area. Where did my twin brother go? I have so much to tell him. I get up and frantically run around and search the area, as if I believed that he had magically resurrected. Of course he hasn't.

My heart is racing, and the silence feels louder than ever. I shout his name again, desperate for a reply, but all I get is a frightened squawk as the swans in the lake swim hurriedly away.

Everything is silent again, and the sun is gleaming on the lake and the pretty green leaves as if nothing had ever happened. My eyes are burning like I'm about to cry, but I can't.

I slump helplessly on the ground when I hear a loud, deep crack, followed by the rustling of leaves. I swivel around, my eyes searching for the familiar figure; but I watch powerlessly as a large branch collapses onto my drawing. A loud thump on my easel seals my fate; my heart breaks as I realize that my painting is ruined, but as the few remaining birds squawk and fly away, I slowly realize that I would have been dead, or at best injured, if I was there a few seconds ago.

I stay on the ground, weak with fear, for a while. If I hadn't seen Theo...

"Thank you." I whisper. I believe he heard it.

I find the energy to get up and walk over to the easel, with no intention of fishing out the painting. I stare at the branch, its large, strong stems holding such delicate leaves that danced in the breeze. Somewhere I find it in me to pull out the drawing, and my hands search under the rough bark. The canvas is there, and I am stunned to find out that it looks okay. In fact, I think, squinting at the paint; it looks better.

The crowned crane I painted has no wings anymore. The paint has been smudged by the bark. The body is textured because of the bark on the tree, and as I am standing there scrutinizing my painting seconds after escaping death, I realize that the bird looks a lot like

Theo. It stands tall, proud of the scars that the tree has created, brave despite having no wings. I am staring, and I smile, and I do not realize I am grinning until my mouth starts hurting.

I walk home, listening to a radio program on birds and their symbolism. The lady speaks slowly and goes in alphabetical order through the species of birds. She reaches C, and she mentions the crowned cranes in Dubai, and how they represent beauty and elegance. I listen to her voice and the samples of bird noises that she plays through my earphones, and I walk through the city holding my canvas like it's gold. The cars zoom by, and the skyline is nothing short of magnificent, lights shining throughout the city like they're imitating the stars in the sky.

I reach my house, and the city is quiet again.

I got the information a week later that my artwork had won the competition. Receiving the painting again, I was able to look at the magnificent, crowned crane once more. It made me realize that I didn't have to worry if no one was there for me, even during my worst times, even if a branch the size of a car fell on me.

My brother will be there for me—brave, proud, striding across the banks of the glimmering lake. I will paint the birds and the plants and the water, letting my brushstrokes speak for what I see, and he will be there for me like I was there for him. I know it.

Salwa, The Shining Star

Ganga Raghunath
Grade 10
Our Own Indian School
Dubai, United Arab Emirates

T*he stars were like tiny jewels in the night sky, and the moon, a pale piece of silk, shone brightly, casting an ethereal glow across the cloudless sky. It gave the grass a serene glow that made me feel at ease. The meadow looked mysterious as we played in it. Suddenly, there was a loud crash, like thunder in my ears. As we looked, we could see bright red flames and smoke rising from it. My heart pounded as my friends started to scream and run in search of safety. But I couldn't move a muscle as I stood there watching in fear, the flames coming closer and closer, their menacing glow swallowing everything in their path. I closed my eyes tightly, hoping this nightmare would end. Suddenly, everything went still. I could no longer hear my friends scream or feel the heat of the flames on my skin. I slowly opened my eyes, expecting to see the flames above me, ready to swallow me whole. But there was nothing, not even a spark of flame to be seen. The stars were gone. There was no longer a moon that could cast its glow to comfort me. The meadow that we were playing in had disappeared, replaced by a dark void that seemed to go on forever. I looked around frantically, searching for my friends. But I saw nothing except the never-ending darkness that seemed to have swallowed me whole. Then there was another crash, louder than the first, and I screamed.*

I woke up shrieking from the nightmare, my heart racing and my hands trembling as I tried to catch my breath. I clung tightly to my soft blanket, desperately needing to escape the darkness that had enveloped me in my sleep. Hearing me scream, Mom came rushing into my room.

"Salwa, are you okay?" Mom exclaimed as she wrapped her arms protectively around me, "You're shaking!"

I heard another crash, somewhere further away this time, and I held tightly onto her soft body. This had been happening for quite some time now, but it had started to become more and more frequent recently. With planes dropping bombs here and there, people dying left and right, you never knew if you are going to be next.

"Ummi, why is this happening to us? What have we done for them to hurt us like this?" I asked.

She looked at me with sad, kind eyes but didn't say anything.

"I'm scared," I murmured under my breath.

"Oh, love!" Mom said, pulling me in closer, "You don't have to be afraid. Nothing will happen to us. The war will soon come to an end, and we can all go back to how our lives were before." But it seemed like she was trying to convince herself more than me.

"Where's Baba?"

"Baba has gone out to get ingredients for the cake," she said smiling.

"Cake? What cake?" I asked, confused, and Mom laughed.

"Your birthday cake, of course!" she said. "It's your birthday today, did you forget?" she laughed.

"Oh!" I said and chuckled.

"And I'm going to bake your cake," she said with a grin that made me laugh.

Another explosion was heard close by, bringing us back to reality.

Mom held me close.

A loud explosion was heard, and the whole building shook. I screamed as the floor under us collapsed and we fell.

"Ummiiiiiiiiiii…..."

"Anne… wake up, wake up!" Mom's voice made me jump out of bed. "You're sweating all over!"

She was right, I was drenched in sweat from head to toe.

"U-ummi… I…." I stuttered.

"Ummi…!? 'I was 'Mom' to you till yesterday!" She said with a baffled gaze.

I looked blankly at her as I tried to remember who and where I was.

Mom laughed and asked, "Did you have a nightmare?"

I shrugged, "I guess so," and smiled back.

"Well…" she said, "You better get ready, or you'll miss your school bus. Ohh! Don't forget that today is International Peace Day. You wouldn't want to miss the celebrations at any cost, right?"

"No, I want to go to school. I won't miss today!"

Schools across Dubai are marking International Peace Day with special assemblies and events, encouraging students to make pledges. Our school has organized a series of activities to celebrate the occasion.

I realize that, under the golden glow of the sun, the United Arab Emirates stands as a beacon of peace. From sending relief to war-torn regions to hosting global peace summits, the UAE's commitment to a harmonious world echoes beyond its deserts, proving that peace is not just an aspiration, but a responsibility.

I quickly got off the bed and dragged myself to the washroom. It was probably due to the news and movies about war I had watched yesterday that gave me such a horrifying nightmare. When I reached

the washroom, I couldn't help but look at myself in the mirror. As I looked on, the reflection of the wall behind me was replaced by a strange darkness. As I kept watching, the water droplets on the mirror began to shimmer, slowly transforming into twinkling stars along with the moon and a vast meadow against the darkness. The stars started to form a pattern that became clearer and clearer as I stared at it, and eventually I realized that it was Salwa's face in front of me. Her eyes looked swollen, and her cheeks were red, indicating that she must have been crying for a long time. My heart swelled with grief for her. The more I stared into the mirror, the more real she began to look.

"Why are people so cruel and selfish sometimes?" Salwa asked.

"I don't know," I said quietly. "If only there was a way to stop all of this and make people understand."

"There is," she said softly. "Share my story. Let people know the truth. Help them see what I see."

"Yes, I will. I'll write about it and make sure people hear your voice."

Relief flickered across her face. The water droplets on the mirror slowly faded, and her reflection blurred, but I no longer felt like she was disappearing. Instead, her strength remained, settling deep within me.

And as I stood there, looking at my own reflection, I knew—her story had become mine to tell.

Intrigue Unveiled: A Royal Guard's Desperate Chase

Noah Jim John
Grade 9
Richard Challoner School
London, England

The room was filled with dazzling light as the sun streamed in through the windows. The sun shone brightly from a clear sky, and the water shimmered with millions of tiny sparkles like diamonds. The breeze rocked softly from side to side, causing the trees to sway in tandem. The sound of happy chirping blended with the aroma of honeysuckle. He opened his eyes, acclimating himself to the bright sunlight. He stood up sluggishly, yawning as he walked to the toilet to wash his face and put on his glasses. Ready for his boring day, he dressed, pulling on his suit and his pointed black shoes. He hurriedly finished his breakfast, shut up the house, and boarded the train for Buckingham Palace. His work was considered legendary or one of a kind. As tourists gasped to discover the palace's genuine inner splendor, the palace stood in awe. People were taking pictures of the palace until their hearts were content because of the happy vibe it exuded. The sun was hot, and the air was heavy, so he felt sleepy as he moved closer to the palace.

The palace walls whispered secrets, each stone a chapter in the novelty of royalty. The towers of the palace reached high like aspirations wrapped in gold. The palace gate guarded the dreams of the generations within. He presented his ID to the guard and asked to be allowed. He served as the head of the royal guard, which meant that he had a very prestigious role. After changing into his royal armor, he heard something. He investigated after hearing what sounded like water dripping; he took no notice of it and thought it was just one of the taps. But then he heard a groaning noise and a repugnant smell in the toilet. He went to go check, astounded he found a dead body! He suddenly felt sick; his mind began to collapse, his thoughts flying across his mind. He staggered to the emergency button; his feet heavy like glass, he could not get rid of the horrifying sight of a dead man. He immediately pushed the button and fell; his eyes flickered as he fainted.

His eyes opened as he felt the harsh light pounding over his eyes. He groaned and tried to sit up. He felt drowsy, unaware of where he was. Someone called to him, saying, "Hello, can you hear me?" He replied, "Yes. Where am I?" He looked up to the voice and saw a nurse who was wearing a familiar badge. He quickly knew that he was in the Royal London Hospital, one of the most prestigious hospitals in London. He knew that something was going on, and he had to figure out what. "Hello. Hello. Hello!" the nurse called. He returned to reality after realizing that he was in a daydream and staring into the wall.

The nurse said to him that he had fainted and hurt his head badly and that he needed to rest for a few days. He took no notice as he wanted to figure out what happened. His memories slowly began to flood in as he could remember what happened before he fainted; he could vaguely remember the dead man and how he pressed the emergency button on time. But he soon thought about the man who died. He knew that he had seen his face somewhere but couldn't place his finger onto who the man was. He knew that he was to call his friends working for the royal guards. He soon told the nurse politely to use a cell phone. The nurse brought it, and he quickly dialed his closest friend, John. He talked about the unprecedented incident. John said to him that the General wanted to see him. He gasped as the General was a bold man. His presence emitted glory and power. His goals were to keep the King alive at all costs.

After he calmed down and changed into some good clothes, he sneaked out of the hospital and went back to Buckingham Palace. On his arrival, he saw a man in black coming out of the changing rooms. The man was running, holding a sharp object, and started to charge at the back exit of the gate. His mind raced as he faced a critical decision: rush to the General or intercept the escaping man. Committing to action, he sprinted like a cheetah, determined to catch the fleeing figure before he vanished. With hair billowing in the wind, the urgency was palpable. Glancing back, the intruder saw the royal guard desperately chasing him down, encouraging him to curse and change direction. Aware he needed to get the royal guard off his tail, the man reached his breaking point, pulled out his gun, and fired warning shots; the chaos of people scattered around in panic. The royal guard, determined to catch the man, started to run faster and pushed through the distraught crowd. He seized the man's black jacket and forcibly brought him to a stop. The man attempted to aim his gun at the royal guard, but a swift kick disarmed him. The royal guard seized this opportunity, took hold of the situation, and instructed the man to go to Buckingham Palace. The tension was palpable as the guard tried to think about how the man was armed in Buckingham Palace. The guard swiftly dialed the police and told them all the details, emphasizing that the man came armed out of Buckingham Palace. The police assured the royal guard and told him that if any other assistance were needed, they would call him immediately. The royal guard sighed with relief but could not help noticing that something was going on. His mind was racing; his thoughts jumbled up; he needed a break.

The London Eye started to spin as the sun glimmered onto it, making a beautiful sight. The London Bridge was a spectacular sight as it opened and closed as boats made their way into the docks. The city was busy with people as they went shopping or grabbing a bite; the rush of people made it feel like a climactic place to be. So, he went into Costa and ordered a drink and a sandwich. The sweet aroma emitting from his caramel latte filled the air, and the sandwich looked buttery, with the bread toasted to a chocolaty brown outside. He smiled to himself as he took a bite, and the crunch of the bread made him warm and fuzzy. He took a sip of his caramel latte, and the sweet taste made him forget about the murder mystery. He enjoyed every single bite of his sandwich and took the caramel latte on his way to Buckingham Palace. He finally reached the palace, and the beauty emitting out and the sheer awe and wonder made tourists stare in fascination. The palace was huge as the sun beamed off it, giving it a warm orange and red color. He showed his ID to the guard, and he went to the changing room. He was thinking about how the man who he chased had a knife and came out of the changing rooms. He made his way towards the door; his heart was beating faster and faster. Sweat was dripping from his brow, and the drops of sweat touched the ground with an eerie sound.

He saw no dead man; he gasped with relief, but he could not help noticing that something was going on. If he didn't kill anyone, what was he doing? He knew he had to investigate further; he came back to reality and started searching the place. He looked through every nook and cranny but still could not find anything. His hopes were down as he had looked everywhere, but suddenly his eye caught something: a red stain on the floor, remarkably close to the door. He wondered if it led anywhere.

He opened the door and found drops of blood on the floor

leading to a dark alleyway. He felt foolish as he didn't realize the blood stains on the floor but saw it led to the sewer. Chills went down his spine as his mind filled with death; his heart pounded every minute, and he felt light-headed. But he knew that lives were taken by these people, so he mustered up the strength to open the sewer and to check where the blood stains had led to. The first thing that hit him was the foul scent of garbage; he gagged, resenting his decision about coming here. The water looked murky, as if something were living there; the water looked green, filled with garbage. The water inhabited frogs that looked like some bacteria was growing out of it. He almost passed out to see a rat with red eyes, looked as if it were about to charge at him. His breathing was hard and increased every second; he followed the blood stains, and it led him to a room.

He felt really confused and scared, with thoughts rushing through his head and his hands shaking with fear. It was like he was about to be pulled into a dark hole. Despite that, he bravely went ahead and saw two guys planning something on a piece of paper. They looked dangerous, and just being near them made him want to hide and forget everything. They had guns on their belts and quickly grabbed them when they noticed him. He didn't know what to do except check out the place and run away.

Carefully avoiding the murky water below, he ran off. Suddenly, a man shouted, "GET HIM NOW!!!" The man's loud voice echoed, making him sprint even faster. His mind was racing, trying to figure out who these guys were and what they wanted. All he knew for sure was that they were connected to the murder mystery like jigsaws fitting into a puzzle. His eyes were desperately searching for an exit or a hiding spot where he could stay calm and not be seen. He wondered about what would happen if the Internal men caught him. But he tried to stay positive when he spotted a rusty steel bar; he knew he could make a weapon out of it. He sighed in relief as he could knock out the two men. He found the perfect spot to do it, holding his breath, hoping they wouldn't notice him. But as soon as he got to his spot, the men saw him, and he started to run. It felt like all his efforts were futile. He needed to lead them out of the sewers. Spotting a ladder, he climbed up and moved a metal plate. The men shot their guns, missing him and hitting the metal. They cursed and climbed the ladder. He was out of the sewer and needed to run. Just as he was about to run, the angry man grabbed his jacket and knocked him out.

His eyes closed, and the last things he saw were the London Bridge fading away in the distance and the men grabbing him.

Beneath the Welsh Sky

Julia Kozuch
Grade 10
Olchfa Comprehensive School
Swansea, Wales, UK

In the midst of a gentle breeze gracefully rolling through the valley of Glynneath, past the tumbling waters of Melincourt Falls, west of the Afan Forest, and down where the River Neath kisses the ocean, sheep joyfully bounce across the lush green meadows. Their cheerful "baas" harmonize with the ancient melody of "Hen Wlad Fy Nhadau," echoing across the timeless landscape. This is a story of how nature nurtures the soul, especially in the land of Gower, a place I am oh-so-lucky to call home. From the Swansea Bay, where the sea glistens in the sunlight, to the sweeping curves of the Loughor Estuary, Gower's beauty is so captivating that even Dylan Thomas couldn't resist immortalizing it in his poetry.

When I was just three years old, I took my first big walk with my family along the towering cliffs of Rhossili, overlooking the majestic Worm's Head. At the time, I didn't know that this place would become a sanctuary of sorts—a place where I would spend many of my teenage days, lost in thought and wonder, with the sea breeze in my hair and the sky wide open above me.

It all truly began when I was ten years old, with a simple wish for a dog. I longed for a furry companion, but my parents were adamant that I was too young, too irresponsible. I tried to prove them wrong, waking up early every Saturday to make them breakfast in bed. For weeks, I kept it up—or rather, three Saturdays. Then I became distracted by the novelty of scented pens my mum had given me. But somehow, my efforts must have worked, because a couple of years later, we adopted the sweetest pooch.

Our canine girl, Olive, and I soon ventured out on walks together. At first, we stuck to the local paths—Cwmdonkin Park and the Swansea Bay. There was nothing Olive loved more than the freedom of running off-lead, her tail wagging joyfully as she raced ahead. By the time I turned twelve, our walks grew more adventurous, taking us to Mumbles, Langland, and Caswell. At first, it was challenging, at least for me, but not for Olive! She had once been a street dog in Portugal, eventually rescued by a Welsh rescue shelter from a Portuguese killing shelter. Olive was a fit girl with an unquenchable passion for running free.

During the school days and winter months, our walks were shorter, less exciting. But whenever the weather permitted, and my study schedule allowed, we'd be out in a flash, exploring the sweet-smelling fields where the wild scent of flowers mingled with the salt of the sea. Eventually, my mum extended my curfew, and though that meant more outings with friends and fewer walks with Olive, my older sister made sure she was never neglected, taking her on grand adventures of their own.

With newfound freedom, I began to explore even farther afield. One sunny summer day, my friends and I packed snacks, a blanket, a flask of tea, and a change of clothes—just in case—and hopped on a bus to Southgate. As we stepped off the bus, our boots sinking into the warm soil, the sun kissed our sunscreen-coated skin, and we giggled in excitement. "What a glorious day for an adventure," I thought.

The path towards Three Cliffs was crowded with locals of the gentlest kind—cows, with their calves by their sides, grazing lazily on the grass. Mothers nudged their little ones, who occasionally paused to nurse. It was a peaceful, pastoral scene, and I felt a sense of awe and gratitude, as if I were witnessing something sacred.

As we neared the edge of the cliffs, the panorama unfolded before us—Three Cliffs, Rhossili, and Oxwich, lined up like jewels, one by one, on the horizon. We scrambled down a steep hill towards a small, rocky bay, secluded and not easily accessible. The tide was coming in, and the water shimmered in the afternoon light, beckoning us. We hadn't planned for swimming, but if there's one thing Welsh weather teaches you, it's to embrace spontaneity. Without hesitation, we shed our jumpers, kept our vests on, and waded into the cool, refreshing water.

Time seemed to stand still as we floated in the sea, the world quiet except for the gentle lapping of the waves. When we emerged, we had no towels, so we sat on a blanket spread over a large rock, letting the sun dry us as we sipped warm tea from our flask. As the sun began its slow descent, casting a golden glow over the landscape, we changed into our spare clothes and started the trek through the woods towards the Gower Heritage Centre, where my mum would pick us up by the Shepherd of Gower, a cozy little shop nestled at the side of a rural road.

That day remains my favorite memory of my Gower adventures. It wasn't just the beauty of the land or the thrill of exploration; it was the sense of connection—to nature, to my friends, and to the simple joys of life.

Nature, particularly Welsh nature, has a way of reminding us to slow down, to embrace the moment, and to cherish the little things— like the warmth of the sun after a swim, the sweetness of tea shared with friends, or the sound of sheep singing in harmony with the land of our fathers. In the hustle of life, it's easy to forget that these small moments are the ones that truly nurture our souls. So, always remember to pause, breathe, and let the world around fill you with wonder and gratitude.

The Moon Paints a Second Stroke

Veronica Antov
Grade 9
Rumsey Hall School
Connecticut, USA

The cerulean hue of the evening air was distilled by the swelling moonlight, the moon's grayish and dimpled face on the brink of waning but plump still. In unison, the choral din of frogs, crickets, and the bumbling annual cicadas met Franklin's ears as the pendulum of his car door swung on its hinges, but he hesitated. His left leg followed, then the new goose bumped into the mixed-media sketchbook that had been resting on the center console. Hobbling slightly across the asphalt, he turned to listen as his car locked and the honking sound of it penetrated nature's cacophony for a brief moment.

His jangly station wagon was the only vehicle parked in the barren lot. State parks close at dusk in New England. He knew his excursion was theoretically illegal but there were never any rangers in a setting so rural; they, unlike Frank, preferred to spend such June nights behind windows and walls, beneath home air unmarred by the perfume of the congealed algae on the stagnant pond. Besides, even if night shifts had been introduced, the greatest repercussion a ranger would give an old man with blanching hair, a bad knee, and a compact set of gouache paints in hand would be a temporary expulsion from the premises, not the fine that the maroon-lettered signs at the entrance promised.

Passing over the wooden bridge, he consulted his cane for steadiness, left knee faltering but never bending more than a few degrees before he rolled his weight to the other side. After a few minutes of prudent walking, Frank came at last to the memorial bench by the waterfall with dedication lettering so deeply permeated by lichens that it made one wonder if its namesake's memory had been entirely lost to the crumbling symbiotes.

He sat, laid out his art supplies so that they sprawled over the empty spot on the bench beside him, and picked at the plastic clasp of the gouache palette with a resolute thumb. Of course, the sky's dome above him was beginning to darken, but if there was but one thing that Frank knew, it was this: the things that fell into the shadows were not always worth drawing.

He knew many who painted the verdant hosta leaves, or who illustrated bouquets of flowers again, again, and again, until the sight of veiny petals or stamen and pistil seemed more familiar even than the placement of the darkening spots on their gnarled artist's hands. No, Frank preferred the negative space on his canvases, preferred lowlighting the white blooms of light with blue and indigo tones, counting the moon's craters, calderas, and plateaus because even though his hearing worsened daily, his eyesight was as keen as a camera lens.

This was perhaps the greatest blessing of his elder life, a coincidental mitigation to salve the plague of his bad knee, he thought. So as the supple brushstrokes began to appear on the paper, Frank forgot the feeling of creaky knuckle joints and long-idle abilities.

Gradually but amply, it began to feel as though he had never really stopped painting, the movements of the paintbrush familiar and his own. He did not try to restrain the satisfied chuckle, nor the furcate crinkles that were forming at the corners of his eyes. Instead, he allowed himself to step into the momentary bliss that made his fingertips tingle with excitement.

This was the joy of an artist, he knew, to render the fruit of one's thoughts and visions into something palpable, tangible even. This was what he had known in the times when he sat in his hemp canvas folding chair, in front of his variform paintings, at countless art fairs. And countless times he had been told by relatives that he would never succeed in this path, but countless times he had retorted, piqued, because there was no worse feeling in his mind than being doubted by others. Then it was a job as a caregiver in a local senior community, and now he was a senior himself and tonight was the first time since his youth that he had painted something, it being the first few hours since his retirement party.

His mind was now void of all the worries that had afflicted him when he still worked, and he had decided he would scrape the film from his box of supplies, buy new paints, and draw inspiration from the state park. When he was finished with the painting, he found himself looking down at the likeness of the landscape in front of him.

The water in the pond was opaque in the descending darkness and reflected the stars' pinpricks as they appeared above. He had captured the gently warped reflection of the moon, with its gray shadows and its aureole, streaked with amethyst because the glow played tricks on his eyes if he looked at it for too long. There were also the contours of the trees, but the main focus was on the moon and stars, as though the dark blue corners of the paper drew in to point at them.

Old indignation flooded Frank's senses, pulsing a rhythm in the vein behind his ear. Yes, he was going to do this more often now in hopes of restoring the talent that once was, and perhaps he could even sell this piece, perhaps someone wanted it above their mantel or their bed's headboard. He envisioned possibilities for how he could sell it, where to obtain a platform or venue so that someone would be bound to purchase it—a market, a fair, a local community art gallery.

Invigoration was what this was, and the excitement made him dizzy. So, he drew in a breath. The breath drew in his sternum. Then the moon fell on his head, the night sky was closing in on his shoulders, and the mobile of the stars became a scattered mess that amalgamated with phosphenes.

The moon was no longer in the sky but a closing crescent that glowed white and slightly lavender in front of his shut eyes, and then it was round, and then it was gone. It is hard to determine whether he experienced any nausea, aches, spasms, or lightheadedness prior to the events of this fateful night. If he had, they were simply dismissed as minor headaches or the onset of arthritis (both of which are common of the aging body). You will be spared any further details of that night, however.

At one point in the morning, someone had called emergency dispatch. The paramedics who arrived noticed that he had no pulse at his wrist, and in turn called the funeral director. Needless to say, the old gentleman never sold his painting but instead it was given to a local gallery where it was admired by many as a great achievement in the art of landscape depictions.

At his funeral, Frank's wife stood to give a tearful eulogy, this painting displayed behind her on the starchy wall of the church. She said nothing of the painting, not looking behind her once, not once so much as glancing at it. She seemed slightly weak at the lectern, but she forced a strained smile as she neared the eulogy's end. Brushing her short, dyed hair up from her eyebrows, she finished it thus: "The moon set on Frank, but he will rise again with it tonight."

Fancy of Fansipan

Ayisha Zeba Riyas
Grade 4
AHI school
Ho Chi Minh City, Vietnam.

I had never seen snow before, so my parents wanted to surprise me by taking me on a holiday to the most northern and coldest part of Vietnam, a country in southeast Asia. We live in Ho Chi Minh City, which is in the southern part of Vietnam. Hanoi is the capital of Vietnam, and you guessed it! We went there too. This is how the vacation began.

At first, we went to Hanoi; I was so excited about the fun ahead, of course! We visited The One Pillar Pagoda, which is the oldest Buddhist temple and shaped like a lotus pedestal. I was amazed to know that this temple is almost one thousand years old and made from wood with artistic details. Just like its name, the temple is built on one pillar in a lake. Next, we went to Tortoise Lake, which is also known as Ngoc Son Temple, with the oldest preserved tortoise body. It's super big! Almost two meters in length. The legend has it that the tortoise cut off its magical front claw and presented it to the king when his army was losing in war, and that golden claw turned into a crossbow and made him win! We could see two such tortoises.

Later in the evening, we went to the Hanoi train street to watch the train pass through the street full of coffee shops. Many small and very beautifully decorated coffee shops are there throughout the street. The customers are guided by shopkeepers well before the train approaches, and street gates are closed and secured by policemen. It is so fascinating to see a big train slowly pass through the colorful coffee shop street. From there, we went to an Indian restaurant; Indian eateries are not so popular in Vietnam, but we have a few of them. This time we had dosa from "Annam" restaurant, and it was so yummy.

In Hanoi, we lived in a hotel in the famous Old Quarter with small shops everywhere! That was a crowded locality, at the same time filled with nostalgic olden Vietnam street styles. And the next day, we went on a Hop-on Hop-off city bus tour, which was impressive! We sat on the top open deck of the bus and could see the whole city on the go. The bus trip covered all the monuments in Hanoi City.

The next day, we had a day trip to Ninh Binh, including a river boat ride. This river is very wide and calm and used to grow the floating rice paddy farm; unfortunately, it was not the season for paddy, and we could not see any. But the slow hand-rowed boat ride was so nice, seeing the true nature in front of us. Hundreds of boats are servicing here, all rowed by Vietnamese ladies; they do this very calmly and with smiles on their faces. As you know, Vietnam has fewer English-speaking people, hence they mostly communicate with simple English words and sign languages to tourists. Sometimes, I see my parents use Google Translate to communicate with them as well.

After Hanoi, we went to Sapa, the highlight of my vacation. Sapa is next to the border of China and Vietnam, so it is very cold there. A sleeper bus trip from Hanoi to Sapa took us to around 4:30 AM in the morning, and there was fog everywhere. We were not able to see anything beyond three meters away; moreover, there was a drizzle of rain as well. We went in the middle of December, so we predicted that it would snow. We were not prepared for such a climate, so we bought gloves and hats right there in Sapa. We lived in Himalaya Hostel, a family-run business by Mr. Huynh. The hotel was small but neat and well-managed. Mr. Huynh shared his amazing bicycle Asian trip starting from Vietnam to Thailand – Myanmar – India – Pakistan, then flying back to India, cycling from Mumbai to Bangalore – Chennai, flying to Singapore. Later, he cycled from Singapore – Malaysia – Thailand, then finally back to Vietnam in one year. This impressed us. He said his favorite country was India, so he lived in India for six months, and he also loves the Himalayas; hence, he named his hostel the same. He told us that he had stopped going around Asia on his bicycle because he has a family to take care of. But he kept up with his passion by riding all around Sapa with visitors.

We heard that there was a traditional village a few kilometers away from our hotel. And I was thrilled to visit. We set off on a taxi and arrived in Cat-cat village. Chill! Is it a village with cats? Nah! It's from the word "Catscat," a French word meaning "There is a beautiful waterfall." The local Vietnamese misspelled it "Cat-cat." We had to walk after our taxi dropped us at the parking area. After a long walk, we arrived at the village! Oh boy! It was so beautiful with greenery and flowers. There was a waterfall with steppingstones, I loved it! There were also horses for photoshoots (I really like horses), and I took pictures on top of one. The people that lived in Cat-Cat village belonged to the Hmong community. On the way back to the hostel, my mom saw some white on a pine tree and screamed that it had started snowing. I went back and checked it closely and found a small piece of cotton someone had left on the tree! We all laughed at mom for her overconfidence about the possibility of a snowy evening. But the trees were almost frozen with waterdrops.

During our stay in Himalaya Hostel, me and my little brother liked playing with Master Bo, a cute three-year-old boy, the son of Mr. Huynh. He was well-adapted to the chilly weather out there, as we were wearing two jackets but this little boy was just roaming around half-naked. He quickly became friends with us and accompanied us for breakfast, bringing his milk bottle along. We still have those small little stickers he pasted on our suitcases. Such a cute little boy he is!

The next place we went was "Fansipan," it is called the roof of Indochina, situated 3,143 meters above sea level. To reach the summit, I had to travel in three types of transport: a monorail from Sapa station to Hoang Lien, a cable car from there to Do Quyen, and lastly, a hill train to the peak. It was so windy and foggy throughout the three-hour journey that we could hardly see the beauty of the terrace rice fields or the huge Buddha statue. But we enjoyed the ride as I was here to enjoy snow, breeze, fog, and chilly wind. At the Fansipan summit, we spent around 15-20 minutes taking photos and feeling the coldest weather I ever experienced. On the way back from the summit, we were supposed to come down by steps, but we didn't feel comfortable in the thick fog to step down 600 steps to the cable station, so my dad decided to buy hill train tickets again to travel back. From there, we followed the same transportation to come down to the base station Sapa.

During our journey down the hills, my dad was explaining about the mountain trekking people who climbed up and came down Fansipan in one day trip. I could see a few guides helping people to do so. I was imagining how hard it would be to climb the top hill by foot, how adventurous they are, isn't it? After Fansipan, we went on a walking tour to a village named Ta Van. It was so surprising to me that all those people in that village spoke incredibly good English and they came in a group and walked along with us for some distance. They were cloth-crafts and souvenir sellers. We understood that they spoke English every day with visitors, and they learned it. At some point in time, they stopped their walk and forced us to buy some clothes from them. Finally, my dad bought a shawl for me, and I liked it well! By this, the Sapa trip ends with lovely memories. From Sapa to Lao Cai by road, Lao Cai to Hanoi by a night train, then back to Ho Chi Minh by flight. Finally, I didn't see the snow, but the trip was impressive with foggy and chilly weather, surrounded by nice people of Sapa; I really loved it. I hope that you will soon visit Sapa and enjoy it also.

Hidden Wonder

Elena Phiri
Grade 11,
City of Hope
Lusaka, Zambia

Eli is a very adventurous girl. She lives in the city of Lusaka, Zambia. Eli has a friend named Taonga. During the summer of 2023, the two planned an adventurous trip to the north of the country, about 600 kilometers from the city.

Upon arrival, Eli heard a booming roar that sounded like a waterfall from a distance. Pushing through bushes and branches with each struggled step, she heard the sound grow louder and louder until she was deafened by the sound of the wonder hidden in the Mbala Hill—as they called the area.

After a glimpse of traditional activities, displayed crafts, and drumbeats, Eli joined the villagers in celebrating the festival feast of the first harvest. The Mambwe people presented various meals to the Chief as a sign of a good harvest. The Visashi was a meal that blew Eli's mind away. It was prepared deliciously from Lumanda (hibiscus sabdariffa) and pounded groundnuts. Dances, songs, and offerings to ancestral spirits and the gods marked the end of the festivities.

The next morning, Eli and Taonga connected with their tour guide, Mr. Sichalwe, who told the girls, "Those who dare walk in the Mwiloola forest never return from its darkness."

Despite the terror they felt, the girls were still determined to uncover the dark one's mystery. As per tradition, they received blessings from the village elders, and their quest began. The trees in the forest seemed to reach for the heavens, clinging to each other as they rose, nearly blocking the light completely. The forest floor was blessed with a wide array of beautiful wildflowers and plants. Among them was a Bougainvillea, which was rare and beautiful. Out of love, Taonga tried to touch the flower, and it gave off its pricky defense. Taonga fell to the ground in screams of awe. Despite Taonga's injury, the girls were not discouraged from discovering Mwiloola's dark mysteries, and they walked further. Sichalwe explained to the girls the do's and don'ts of the forest.

No sooner had they begun than the girls heard a hollow sound of what seemed to be water. Cautiously, they walked closer and closer to the source of the sound, which began to resemble that of a waterfall. As the girls trailed the thundering sound, leaving Sichalwe behind, the trees seemed to tower higher with branches twisting and gnarled like grasping fingers. The forest floor was covered in a thick carpet of leaves and branches, and the air was thick with the scent of damp earth and decaying leaves. The feeling of being watched had its claws around the girls in a tight hold as the trees moved closer together, choking out any light. The hollowing sound of water grew louder and louder with each struggled step, as the girls pushed through bushes and branches until they were completely deafened by the thunderous

roar of the waterfall before their eyes in all its immense glory. Frozen in amusement and amazement, the girls stared at the veils of white water falling in a never-ending series between two cliffs, covered in lush green vegetation and wildflowers. Trees surrounding the falls were graced by different species of birds, each chirping their own unique call.

The two were brought back to reality by the loud call from Sichalwe, who was also amazed upon sighting the falls.

"Who knew something this phenomenal could be found in Mwiloola!" Taonga expressed after taking in the mesmerizing beauty of the falls.

Sichalwe suggested that they take a refreshment break and perhaps discover more about the falls and its surroundings. After refreshments, the girls began their exploration of the fall's surroundings. As they walked along the riverbank, Taonga noticed fish moving about in the water.

"Eli, hurry! There are fishes in the water!" Taonga said, pointing at the clear water.

After spotting many different types of fish, the girls decided to walk nearer to the falls, whose spray due to its forceful crush at the bottom began to dampen their clothes.

As the girls enjoyed the spray of the falls, Sichalwe told them that they better head back to the village before dark. Eli agreed with her, as they would easily find their way back while it was bright.

"The fish are so lucky to stay in such a beautiful paradise," Taonga said with envy.

As they walked further away, the girls decided to each pick a stone to keep part of the forest with them. They searched for the perfect stones until they found just the right ones. Worry spread across Sichalwe's face as he told the girls they might have taken the wrong path. After trying several different paths, Sichalwe and the girls only seemed to get deeper into the forest. After a while, Sichalwe suggested that they settle for the night. Taonga was perplexed at the idea of sleeping on damp earth and the insects in the forest, but soon gave in, expressing that she was an adventurer.

Early the next morning, shortly after the girls began walking, they arrived at a familiar path which led back to Bougainvillea, where Taonga warned them to stay away from the plant, causing both Sichalwe and Eli to laugh. As Eli and Taonga followed Sichalwe back to the village, they put together their story about the falls, while Eli and Taonga narrated their experience. Eli had an intense urge to uncover more wonders in the forests of Zambia. From the rivers that stream wild, the trees that stretch to touch the heavens, to flowers that color the land and birds that color the skies, and animals that grace the landscapes in Zambia. This is the beauty that graces the land of work and joy.

The Unveiling

Tatenda B Tokwe
Progress Christian School
Gweru, Zimbabwe

As the sun began to set, its red gloom flooding the African landscape, I watched from the window of the car, young boys guiding the small herd of cattle towards the kraal. The journey from the city had taken us two hours. As we arrived at the homestead, I saw so many people, young and old, coming to greet us.

"This is Brighton, my youngest son," I overheard my mother saying to two old grannies.

"Oh!! A tall young man resembling his grandfather," said one of the grannies.

"Now that you have all arrived from the city, the rituals will begin this evening," another of the grannies told my mother.

Some two months earlier, I recalled my mother telling us about the visit to the rural home.

"Do you still know where your grandparents lie buried?" she had asked me, gazing into my eyes. I had expressed ignorance and lack of knowledge, but then she told me everything about how this ceremony was important to our family. She had said these were occasions when we would meet so many relatives and get to know each other. Today, I realized this to be true as we walked towards the graveyard. We were there now.

"Herbert, we are cleaning your home; your children are here, and we are honored," said one of the grannies.

"Now allow us to sweep this place and make it tidy for the big occasion tomorrow," the thin-skinned granny remarked as she continued speaking, some of which I did not understand.

Later, we were back at the homestead eating the evening meal. Women were at fireplaces, and pockets of men sat around in groups on wooden stools, some telling African stories while others imbibed in African draught beer, throwing jokes here and there all under the watchful eye of the evening summer moon.

The following morning, I was awoken by religious singing. I dashed to the yard and followed the prayers. It was not long when we all entered the round African thatched hut where more prayers were conducted before marching towards the graveyard amid ululation and singing. I heard the word "Hossana" and felt some joy.

Arriving at the graveyard, I saw a big, bright banner with photos of my late grandfather and grandmother. Could this be one of their photos, I thought to myself as it looked like they had returned to earth, and they were with us. I felt like shedding tears. A heart-touching religious event drowned the whole place as the unveiling began. First, the two old grannies knelt before my late grandfather's grave to remove the veil, followed by relatives of my late grandmother doing the ritual at my late grandmother's tombstone.

"Now that the tombstones have been unveiled, let us bow our heads and pray," announced the elderly priest. After ten minutes of prayers, all relatives took time to greet and laugh as they slowly trickled back at the homestead. The unveiling was over, and what an experience I had witnessed. As I joined the others, I could hear a voice telling me to narrate this experience to my future children.

SPECIAL THANKS

Nargish Khambatta (Principal GEMS Modern Academy, Dubai and Senior Vice President-Education), Jennifer Branch (President, IASL), Fredrik Ernerot (Vice-President IASL), Katy Manack (Former President, IASL), Sydney Atkins (Associate Principal, GEMS Modern Academy), John Gomes (Vice-Principal, GEMS Modern Academy, Dubai), Michael Dowling (Director, ALA), Toshiko Malhotra (Head of Primary, GEMS Modern Academy), Dr. Luisa Marquardt (IFLA Division E Deputy Chair 2024-2025) Rome - Italy, Muralee Thummarukudy (Director of the Coordination Office of UN Convention to Combat Desertification), Zakir Hussain (Vice President of the International Association of School Librarianship) Switzerland, Anna Cascone (Italy), Virginie Laude (France), Ekaterina Sosulnikova (Russia), S.M. Moinul Abedin (DPS STS School, Dhaka, Bangladesh), Hellon Chan (Hong Kong), Sophia Adeyeye (Nigeria), Dr. Maria F. Nicolau (Head Librarian, Binus School, Indonesia), Valerie Rupe DiLorenzo, Dr.Juliet Caroline (USA), Liezl Cabantog (Philippines), Marianna Pataki (Hungary), Sanda Ignjatovic (Serbia), Dr. Maya Abdul (Head Librarian, Malaysia), Mijin (Vietnam), Olga Salamakhina (NIS Kokshetau, Kazakhstan), Melanie Wood (Librarian, China), Antonija (IASL Regional Director - Europe), Sabu Hariharan (New Zealand), Amanda Bjorling (Librarian, Luxembourg), Pavel Silenchuk (Luxembourg), Radha Padmanabhan (Lesotho), J.K. Vijayakumar (Antigua), G.Krishnakumar (Finland), Pramod Lal, Victor Davidson (Australia), Anna C (Italy), Fr. Saju Aruvelil (Argentina), Shaji Thomas (Brazil), Girikrishnan, Ashwathy (Germany), Rehana (Holland) Eric Kwaswo Afranie (Ghana), L.H. Wajira Ranjika Silva (Sri Lanka), Rajesh M.V (Maldives), Aboo Anthroth (Lakshadweep), K.P. Sudheera (India, Kerala), Pika Amith Eynullayeva (Azerbaijan), Farhat Fatima (Pakistan), Surur Kamel Hussein (Iraq), Ritesh Dhanak, Vinaya Venugopal, Hebatallah Tarek, Dr. Joelle Joseph Filfili, Uurmi Ghosh, Julia Robertson, Rumana Aziz, Sindhu Joseph, Deeksha Handa, Aarti Seth, Shelly Das, Sangeeta Sahney, Sumaiya Vajawala, Razaz Elshafie, Eman Ibrahim Gadalla, Anjana Ninan, Mohammed Salim, Jignyasa Patel, Mithra Bharucha, Judy Mendes, Sharon Francisca Lobo,

Cheryl Menzies (GEMS Modern Academy, Dubai), Lancy Varghese (Dubai), Michelle Deegan, Sabu Hariharan (New Zealand), Ayesha Rashed Al Maqoodi Alfalasi (Sharjah), Christene (Uganda), Dorothy Phiri (Zambia), Dr. Nour Abuateyh (Jordan), Rehana Hussain (The Netherlands), Rajesh Kanjirakkadan (Tanzania), Jayarati Gurung (Nepal), Tokwe Hosea (Zimbabwe), Manoj Kodiyath, Prasanth CK (Dubai), Pavithran Nambiar (Qatar), Sujith Gangadharan (Bangalore, India), Rajani Roshan, Ammara Kulsum, Angela Roshan (GEMS Modern Academy), Litton Smlf (Singapore), Sabeena M Sali (Saudi Arabia), Ayse Yuksel-Durukan, Sevgi Arioglu (Turkey), So-Young, Lee (South Korea), Ella Bajkowska-Redfern (Wales,UK), Sajith Shankar (Kenya). Harikrishnan (Djibouti), Harish J Nair (Benin Republic, Africa).